"You don't seem to be yourself tonight. Is something wrong?"

"I guess I'm jus
once we're awa...ce," she hedged.

It was a poor excuse for an explanation, ...e could hardly tell him that she was terrified by the fast-approaching deadline that awaited her.

"I know," she continued, "it's silly, right?"

"Yeah, it's silly. You'll be fine. *We'll* be fine."

Tami took a step closer to Keaton and put a hand on his shoulder.

Keaton reacted to her touch and turned to her with a face that could have been carved from granite.

"Keaton?"

His pupils flared and she heard the slight hitch in his breath before he reached for her and dipped his head to take her lips in a kiss that seared away any thought of anything or anyone else.

* * *

Scandalizing the CEO by Yvonne Lindsay
is part of the Clashing Birthrights series.

Dear Reader,

Bribery and corruption make for very uncomfortable bedmates in *Scandalizing the CEO*, book two in my Clashing Birthrights series. After being set up by her ex-boyfriend to take the fall for his embezzlement, Tami Wilson is forced to accede to her father's demands to make things right. This leads her directly into the sphere of Keaton Richmond: a man who will do anything to protect his family and who trusts no one from outside his inner circle.

Researching this book brought many challenges, not least of which were from a legal and investigative perspective, and I would like to acknowledge the assistance from my more experienced sources on "Legal Fiction" and "Cops and Writers" Facebook groups. Any mistakes I've made are very definitely my own.

One of the aspects of my research was for the setting of the outdoors experience where Tami and Keaton learn to get to know one another better. A writing friend lives in beautiful Sedona, and I've been totally wooed by the photos she posts of her hikes in the area. The countryside is spectacularly beautiful and Sedona is definitely on my wish list of places to visit when the world reopens to travel once more. Pushing Tami and Keaton together in such an amazing setting was a great deal of fun, and I hope you'll enjoy reading about it in *Scandalizing the CEO*.

If you haven't read it yet, please also look out for book one in the new series *Seducing the Lost Heir* and remember, if you want to stay in touch I can be reached on Facebook (yvonnelindsayauthor) or Twitter (@yvonnelindsay), or you can contact me via my website, yvonnelindsay.com.

Happy reading!

Yvonne

YVONNE LINDSAY

SCANDALIZING THE CEO

Recycling programs for this product may not exist in your area.

ISBN-13: 978-1-335-23272-4

Scandalizing the CEO

Copyright © 2021 by Dolce Vita Trust

This edition published by arrangement with Harlequin Books S.A.

For questions and comments about the quality of this book, please contact us at CustomerService@Harlequin.com.

Harlequin Enterprises ULC
22 Adelaide St. West, 40th Floor
Toronto, Ontario M5H 4E3, Canada
www.Harlequin.com

Printed in U.S.A.

Award-winning *USA TODAY* bestselling author **Yvonne Lindsay** has always preferred the stories in her head to the real world. Married to her blind-date sweetheart and with two adult children, she spends her days crafting the stories of her heart. In her spare time she can be found with her nose firmly in someone else's book.

Books by Yvonne Lindsay

Harlequin Desire

Wed at Any Price

Honor-Bound Groom
Stand-In Bride's Seduction
For the Sake of the Secret Child

Marriage at First Sight

Tangled Vows
Inconveniently Wed
Vengeful Vows

Clashing Birthrights

Seducing the Lost Heir
Scandalizing the CEO

Visit her Author Profile page at Harlequin.com, or yvonnelindsay.com, for more titles.

You can find Yvonne Lindsay on Facebook, along with other Harlequin Desire authors, at Facebook.com/harlequindesireauthors!

To the amazing and wonderful
Kim Standridge Boykin.
Thank you for sharing your insights and
pictures of your exquisitely beautiful home.

One

"This is where you'll be working. Take a seat."

Begin with the end in mind, Tami told herself as she settled at the desk she'd just been shown to by the HR staffer who had greeted her on her arrival at Richmond Developments this morning. It was a policy that had led her to start many projects, not all of them successful, but she'd always maintained it was a good stepping-off point.

Tami tugged at the unfamiliar skirt she was wearing. More into jeans or leggings and a T-shirt, herself, the suit she'd donned today screamed corporate chic at the same time as she'd screamed internally at the cost of it. Not because she couldn't afford it, but because of the meals that amount of money could have provided at the shelter for displaced families that was run by the charity where she used to work. Her stomach clenched hard at the memory and the reason why she'd been forced to leave. The same reason she was here now.

When her father had made his demands clear, her mom had smoothly stepped in and ensured she had the appropriate props for her new role. Clothes, shoes, makeup, manicure, hair—even a new smartphone. The list was endless. The end would justify the means, she reminded herself, and she could always return the Chanel suits to her mom to add to the collection for her next charity auction. The same could be said for the silk blouse she was wearing today, which was the same hue as Tami's hazel eyes.

The impeccably groomed HR staffer smiled but Tami noticed it didn't so much as crinkle the skin at the corners of the woman's cold blue eyes. Was everyone here like that? Remote and unfriendly? This job might be harder than she thought. Then another thought occurred to her. Was this woman the mole her father had within Richmond Developments? The one that had assured her of her own position here so she could spy on one of the joint CEOs? It wasn't as if she could actually ask her, though, was it?

"We try to run a paperless office in as far as it is possible here, so any note-taking will be on your issued device or your computer. You'll be given your passwords by IT in the next half hour or so. Guard them carefully and share them with no one. Is that understood?"

Tami felt the words like a punch to the gut. No

one knew about the event that had driven her here—well, no one except her, her dad, the charity that was stripped of its bank-account contents and the pond-scum-sucking lowlife who'd stolen the funds. Okay, so *some* people knew. But with that very basic, common-sense admonition, Tami had again been reminded of exactly how stupid she'd been allowing her boyfriend to use her laptop. *Ex*-boyfriend, she corrected silently. She swallowed against the lump that had thickened her throat.

"Don't worry. I take security very seriously," she answered. *Now*.

She'd learned her lesson the hard way when her ex-boyfriend, Mark Pennington, who was the director of Our People, Our Homes, the charity they both worked for, had borrowed her laptop, accessed her banking code for duplicate authorization and then subsequently cleaned out the bank accounts. The bitter truth of his betrayal, the absolute abuse of her trust, still made her feel physically ill. And, while Tami was the kind of person who could forgive a lot, she'd never forgive Mark for stealing from those so much less fortunate, or for making her go to her father for help. She felt a personal responsibility to the charity and had offered to repay the missing two and a half million from a trust fund her grandmother had established for her. The trouble was, her father was one of the trustees administering the fund and he'd made it clear to the other trustees that she was incapable of taking control of it as an adult—all because of a few rebellious choices when she was a teenager. But he'd agreed to distribute the necessary funds to her if she did what he asked and spied on his biggest rival.

"Good," Ms. HR continued. "Mr. Richmond will be here shortly. He mostly sees to his own needs in the office, but be ready to attend any meetings immediately. He'll need you to take notes and load them to the cloud that you will share with him alone. Is that clear?"

"As glass," Tami answered, resisting the urge to add a salute and heel click at the same time.

As if the woman could sense her irreverence, she gave Tami another cold, hard stare before nodding. "If you need me, you can reach me by telephone or email. My details are in the company directory in your computer."

"Thank you, I'm sure I'll be fine."

The woman cocked a perfectly plucked and outlined eyebrow. "You'd need to be better than fine. Mr. Richmond delivers the best at all times and that's exactly what he expects from his inner circle, too."

"Duly noted. Is that all?" Tami said as officiously as she could. No small feat for someone who'd rather be handing out meals to families or calming a confused child while her mom got some sleep on a cot nearby.

"For now. Have a good day."

The moment she was alone, Tami sank down into the chair at her desk. At least it was comfortable, she noted as she gave it a spin.

"'Mr. Richmond delivers the best at all times and

that's exactly what he expects from his inner circle, too,'" she muttered as she looped around a second and a third time. "Well, how's this for a circle?" She spun once more for the hell of it.

There was a sound behind her and she rapidly put her expensively well-shod feet in their boringly practical pumps down to the carpeted floor, bringing herself to a halt as she turned back around. A man, in what was clearly a bespoke dark suit, stood in front of her. Impeccably dressed, from his perfectly shined shoes all the way up to his immaculately groomed hair. Even the light beard on his face had not a whisker out of place.

"Ms. Wilson, I presume?" he said in a deep, well-modulated voice that turned her insides into molten honey.

Wait, that wasn't supposed to happen. She was off men for good, maybe even forever, wasn't she? Especially after the last one. But, despite having been caught out, quite literally, fooling around on the job, and despite that weird reaction to the tone of his voice, Tami managed to gather her wits and stand up to greet him.

"Yes," she answered with the smile she'd been practicing in the mirror all weekend as she offered her hand. "Please, call me Tami. And you're Mr. Richmond?"

He looked at her with clear gray eyes that felt as though they were staring right through her. He hesitated a moment before taking her hand. The second he touched her, Tami felt a quiver of highly inappropriate interest ripple through her body. One that intensified into a distinct tingle that headed to her lady parts as his lips spread into a smile of welcome. He let go of her hand and Tami fought the urge to rub hers down over her thigh. That man needed to license that smile, she thought privately.

"I'm Keaton. There are two Mr. Richmonds here in the office and we're identical twins, so you'll need to figure out how to tell us apart. You'll be reporting to me, and only me. Is that understood?"

She fought the urge to roll her eyes. What was it with everyone here with all the rules? It was going to make her job so much harder. These people needed to lighten up. Although, given the well-publicized drama when Keaton's father suddenly died last Christmas and it was revealed that he had a whole secret life on the other side of the country, including another wife and kids, maybe she could understand their need to be sticklers for convention.

"Ms. Wilson?" he prompted.

"Oh, yes, sorry. Of course," she said, feeling totally flustered at being caught not paying attention, again.

Heat suffused her cheeks and she just knew her skin had gone all blotchy. *Way to go on making a good first impression*, she told herself.

Keaton watched as his new EA changed color. Judging by their interchange so far, he was beginning to wonder if he'd done the right thing in leaving the appointment solely to Monique in HR. Perhaps she hadn't been quite as meticulous in her vetting procedures as usual. Or maybe it was merely an indication of the caliber of person now applying to work here at Richmond Developments, that Tami Wilson was the best of the bunch. Since the scandal involving his father's second family and the damage the publicity had done to their family name, not to mention the company stock, morale had been low at the office. Several key staff had left, hence the recruitment of the woman standing in front of him doing her best impression of a beet.

"Perhaps you could come in to my office and we can go over a few things together."

"Do you want me to make notes?" she asked.

He watched as she caught her lower lip between her teeth. His gaze locked on to the lush fullness of that part of her and he was momentarily transfixed. Keaton gave himself a mental shake and dragged his eyes upward to hers. Hazel. He couldn't remember the last time he'd met someone with precisely that shade of green-brown, nor with such thick dark lashes. Natural? he wondered. None of his business, he reminded himself firmly and gathered his thoughts to answer her question.

"Unless you have a perfect memory, it would probably be a good idea. At least until we get a better grip of how we're going to work together."

Or even if they were going to continue to work together, he realized. She was distracting. Far prettier than the male assistant he'd had previously, and wearing a suit and shoes that were definitely not straight off the rack. She was worse than distracting, to be honest. He did not need or want distraction. He and his siblings, Logan and Kristin, were fighting to keep Richmond Developments going, and with what he was about to tell Tami, he wondered if he shouldn't just assign her elsewhere within the company because the idea of spending the next week alone with her sounded like his worst nightmare.

He moved into his office and after a short while, Tami followed. He settled behind his desk and gestured to her to sit down in one of the chairs opposite him. She did so, unconsciously hitching up the hem of her skirt just a little. Try as he might, he couldn't help but appreciate the shapely thigh, highlighted by the sheerest of black stockings, that she exposed with the action. She tapped a stylus against the phone device she'd brought in with her. Like her outfit, it was sleek and expensive-looking. Clearly, Ms. Wilson wasn't short of a penny. He only hoped she worked as hard as she obviously shopped.

But, it occurred to him, it also wasn't the standard issue to Richmond Developments staff. Since pretty much everything in their offices was conducted electronically and maintained within a strictly operated company cloud, he could only assume she hadn't been allocated her own device yet and that the phone was her own. He'd have to ensure that she understood that the moment she began to record company information electronically, it became the property of Richmond Developments. They couldn't afford to have any of their property, intellectual or otherwise, inadvertently shared with the outside world. Their business rivals were circling like sharks, waiting for them to crumble in what was a difficult and highly competitive market.

He decided to tackle the issue of the phone immediately, so he picked up his own tablet from the desk and logged in to a blank page. It wasn't strictly protocol to share his device, but the document would upload to their shared cloud and she'd be able to access it from her computer and her own company-issued device once she had been given her passwords from IT.

"Here, rather than clutter up your personal phone with company information, use my device," he said firmly, handing it over the desk toward her. "If you scribe in that window, it'll convert your handwritten notes to text and we'll both be able to access them after our discussion."

"Oh, okay, sure. My previous role was with a charity and we were a lot less strict on note-taking procedures."

She smiled as she said it, but he saw the question in her eyes. It surprised him.

"We used to be less careful, but we recently decided to tighten everything up here. Anyway, tell me a little about yourself," he began. "Exactly where were you working before you came here and what made you want to work for us?"

"Oh, um… I was working for a charity that specifically assists displaced people. We not only provide kitchens and shelters, but also work toward placing our people in actual homes. It was challenging and rewarding work and I enjoyed it, but—" She swallowed and took in a deep breath. "It was time to change. As to working with Richmond Developments, it's a well-established company with a strong reputation for integrity and an eye for detail. Who wouldn't want to work with you? While my work with the charity allowed me a lot of diversity within my role, I see this as an opportunity to hone my talents in organization and project development, while bringing my personality and interpersonal skills to the table."

They were fine words, but Keaton couldn't help feeling there was a lot there that she didn't say. Like, if she enjoyed the charity work so much, why had she left?

"And what do you do with your spare time?"

She laughed then. A charming chuckle that sent a flurry of warmth spiraling through him. Keaton found himself involuntarily smiling in response.

"Oh, spare time isn't something I indulge in often. The work at the charity took up much of my spare time and I like to volunteer where I can, as well. Overall, I like to be useful and offering support to those in need is deeply fulfilling. But, during the evenings I'm not helping at the shelter, I find it relaxing to knit. Again for charitable causes like the homeless shelters and animal rescues."

"Knit? Isn't that something older people do?"

Tami arched a brow at him and a pitying smile quirked at the side of her mouth. "Older people? Isn't that a little ageist, Mr. Richmond? I thought your company prided itself on inclusiveness."

It was gentle, but she was definitely chiding him and he had the grace to acknowledge her censure.

"I'm sorry, yes, it was inappropriate of me. And, please, do call me Keaton. To be honest, I don't think I've ever known anyone who knits. It's certainly not a skill my mother possesses."

"It's wonderful," she said, her eyes lighting with enthusiasm. "You get to work with color and texture, and see something grow from a straight line into a garment that can be worn, enjoyed and be functional at the same time. What's not to love about it?"

"Well, when you put it that way..." He laughed in response.

She was different, that was for sure. If he wasn't careful, he had no doubt she'd be giving him knitting lessons—she was so animated about it. He was impressed that she hadn't been afraid to call him out on the ageist comment. There weren't many employees here that would do that, be it existing or new. And she hadn't hesitated. That was a good sign as to her personality, despite the fact he'd caught her fooling around on her chair when he'd arrived. Maybe she would be a breath of fresh air in the place. Goodness knew they needed something.

But they weren't there to have fun and games, he reminded himself. They had a business to bring back to its former strength—and beyond—which meant that he had to focus on the tasks at hand.

"Okay, well, if you slide the stylus from the top

there," he said, gesturing to where she could extract the tool that would help her write on the screen, "we can get started."

He waited until she'd done so before continuing.

"You may be aware that Richmond Developments has been in a state of flux since the death of our CEO, my father, Douglas Richmond. His sudden passing and the revelation of a second family gave the media way more fodder to create bad press against the company. We can't afford any additional slanted reporting against the company or those working within it."

An uncomfortable expression crossed her face and she nodded carefully before speaking. "I had read about your father's death. My condolences on your family's loss. It must have been very difficult for you all."

Keaton felt every muscle in his body tense and let go again. So she'd obviously read the newspapers or heard the gossip. At least he didn't have to revisit that again by explaining the situation in further depth to her.

"We are currently in a rebuilding phase," he said firmly. "Part of that phase is strengthening relationships. First, within our company, then subsequently, with our suppliers and clientele."

"That sounds like a very good plan."

He allowed himself a smile. "Thank you for your approval."

And just like that, she colored up like a beet all over again.

"I didn't mean to sound condescending," she said, obviously flustered.

"You didn't," he reassured her before continuing. "We are in a unique position, you and I. We don't have a working history together, which is problematic in some ways, but in others it offers us a blank canvas from which to build. On the recommendation of the consultant we hired to target boosting staff morale, we are running structured team-building experiences across the company. As you and I are a team of two, we will be conducting ours together and using that time to ensure the wilderness experience that was chosen will meet our requirements as a team builder for both Richmond Developments and DR Construction. We are working to build a strong working relationship between the two companies and that starts with its employees. The other teams will be larger, obviously, based on their department sizes."

A small *V* pulled between Tami's dark eyebrows as she frowned. "A team of two. Just us. Together," she repeated.

"Yes. I agree it's not ideal, as we don't even know one another, let alone know how we will work together, however, as one of the CEOs I have to be seen to be doing the right thing so we will embark on our team-building experience first thing tomorrow. It's a good opportunity for us to discover one another's strengths and weaknesses, while testing out the experiences the course has to offer. Another two groups will meet us there on Saturday morning and we'll complete aspects of the course with them."

The frown deepened. "Tomorrow? Isn't that rather soon? I don't even know what this will entail. What if I don't feel comfortable with this idea? As you so rightly pointed out, we don't even know one another. And you mentioned wilderness?" Her voice raised several octaves on that last word. "I'm a city girl. I don't have any wilderness experience at all."

"Nor I. Which makes it the perfect opportunity for us to rectify that. As I said, we leave tomorrow. I'll arrange a driver to collect you from your home at oh-five-hundred hours."

Tami squeaked a sound of shock. "That's five a.m., right? Don't you think that's a bit early?" She gave a nervous little laugh. "I'm really not my best until at least eight."

"Tami, I'm sure I don't need to remind you that as a new employee, you are on a trial period, per the terms of the contract you signed. Either of us can terminate that contract. If you're telling me you don't wish to work here then please feel free to leave."

She looked at him then, her green-brown eyes widened in shock. "No!" she blurted, before composing her features. "I'll be ready at five a.m., as required. Do you have a packing list?"

"I do, as it happens." He slid a sheet of paper across the desk.

"I thought you preferred a paperless office," she commented before covering her mouth with her hand. "My apologies again. I sometimes tend to speak before I think."

"Well, then, that should make our time away very interesting, because I, too, have been accused of that. Sounds like it's something we can work on together, right?"

She nodded and picked up the list. He watched as she skimmed the items.

"Hiking boots? Backpack for luggage, day pack for day trips? Evening wear? That's an interesting list. Exactly where are we going?"

"Sedona."

"But that's—"

"In Arizona. About a three-hour flight, which we'll undertake in the company jet, and then I understand we have a forty-five-minute drive to our destination."

"Well, okay. I can make sure I have all of this by tomorrow."

"I'm aware that you may not have everything required immediately at hand, so I suggest you spend the balance of this morning on orientation here at the office, then leave at midday to purchase whatever supplies you don't already have. Make sure to forward your receipts to Accounting. They will reimburse you."

She nodded and looked at him from under her lashes. Those eyes. They were intensely staring at him as if she was trying to read his mind and through to the very essence of him. It made him uncomfortable and he didn't like that she could have that effect on him. He shifted his gaze so he was looking at a point just past her ear, inwardly shocked that he could be unsettled by something as innocent as a look. Was it that he was too suspicious these days? That he now saw villains at every twist and turn of each day?

He knew Tami Wilson would have been thoroughly vetted by HR before her appointment, so why did he feel this prickle of unease about her? Was it because she was so attractive? However she looked, it should make no difference to him whatsoever. He'd done the whole office-romance thing once before and been badly burned when his then-fiancée had slept with his twin brother. Granted, she'd initially thought Logan was him, but the fact remained their relationship had been destroyed, and while all three of them continued to work together, there was an element of strain there now that affected everyone around them. He sure as hell wasn't going to set foot on that road again, no matter the appeal of the person working with him.

He bent his head to his desk and clicked a few buttons on his keyboard, then looked back up to her again.

"Any questions, Ms. Wilson?"

"Please, do call me Tami, and no. I think I have everything I need here."

"Good, then if you'll hand me back the tablet, I'll ensure that any notes you made are sent to our cloud. You'll be able to access that from your desktop and from your own tablet when it's issued."

She passed his device back to him. Their fingers brushed. It was the slightest of contacts, but it made everything inside his body clench tight. Instinctive fight-or-flight reflex, he told himself as she withdrew her hand and rose from her chair. Attraction, another more insidious voice whispered in his ear. He rid himself of the suggestion instantly, even though he couldn't help but watch her as she walked from his office to her desk. The fit of her skirt enhanced the sweet curve of her backside and her jacket was nipped in enough at the waist to showcase a perfect hourglass figure. And he was being all kinds of fool looking at her and noticing these things, he reminded himself. He swiveled his chair to gaze out the window at the rain streaming down the glass, all but obscuring the cityscape beyond.

The outdoors course was going to be tough enough without the added complication of Ms. Tami Wilson. He wondered how they'd cope having to rely on each other through each demanding day... and night.

Two

As their plane began its descent to the airport, Tami sat as far from her window as her seat belt would allow. While she was quite certain the stunning view of the cliffs, some distance from the mesa where the airport was situated, was incredibly beautiful, she didn't need to see them from above—or from the side—as their plane raced toward the ground.

The journey in the Richmond company jet had been a comfortable one, except for the proximity of her boss sitting directly opposite her for the journey, and the uncomfortable fact that she hated flying. It had become unsettling to find his eyes on her a couple of times. It wasn't as if he was staring—it was more that she was so hyperaware of his presence that if he turned in her direction she knew it instantly.

She'd never thought that good peripheral vision was a problem, until now. Now she wished she wasn't as keenly attuned to his every movement, or the sighs of frustration that came from deep within him as he scanned whatever was on his tablet screen.

"I thought we weren't supposed to bring work away on this jaunt," she commented.

"I'm trying to get as much completed as I can before we land. Once we're on the tarmac this will be locked away on the aircraft and we are to be incommunicado with the outside world as much as we can. Even mobile-phone coverage is going to be patchy."

"That sounds…" She struggled to find the right word. She suspected that *antediluvian* would not be particularly well-received. "A challenge," she said lamely.

He snorted a small sound that might have been indicative of humor, but it could as easily have been derision. A sudden drop in the aircraft's altitude made her hands tighten on the armrests.

"Don't worry, it's just a downdraft," Keaton quickly assured her. "Quite normal for this runway, I'm told."

"Normal. Right."

He gave her a quick smile. "It'll be okay. We only hire the best at Richmond Developments, and that includes our pilots."

The best? Did he think that included her? A pang of guilt tugged at her ever so slightly, but she clamped down on the thought. She felt the plane drop farther, and with the unwilling compulsion of someone facing certain doom, she turned her attention to the window just as the wheels hit the tarmac. Her knuckles went white as she tightened her grip on the armrests and she forced herself to recite the mantra she'd trained herself to use when flying. Bit by bit, she willed her body to relax back into her seat as the plane rapidly slowed. When she looked forward again, she saw Keaton's eyes firmly fixed on her. No looking away this time.

"You didn't mention you're a nervous flyer," he said with a note of compassion in his voice she hadn't heard before.

"It's not something I'm proud of and I've come a long way in recent years. There was a time I couldn't even set foot in an airport without turning into a wobbly lump of jelly."

"Then you've come a long way. If I hadn't been watching you, I would never have noticed."

So he had been watching her—she knew it. Thinking it and knowing it were definitely two different things. And knowing it made something pull deep down inside her.

He continued. "My mom is a nervous flyer, too. Perhaps, when we return to Seattle, you could spend some time with her and explain the techniques you use."

Tami swallowed back her anxiety as the plane taxied toward the airport terminal. Helping others was what she loved to do most of all. Maybe it was her nature, but sometimes she suspected it had more to do with focusing on other's needs so that she didn't have to consider her own.

"Sure, I'd love to share my coping techniques if I can. No guarantees that what works for me will work for her, though."

"Understood," he responded with a nod.

The aircraft came to a complete halt and the pilot informed them they were free to disembark when they were ready. Tami watched as Keaton shut down his tablet and rose to stow it in a neatly hidden cupboard beside his chair.

"That's nifty," she said, gesturing to the hidden compartment.

"One of the perks of being able to customize your corporate aircraft. You can make the most of the nooks and crannies the shape of the fuselage provides. Come on, let's go. Once we have our packs we can pick up our rental and head out to the camp."

Tami felt a frisson of nerves. She'd never been camping, although the list of items she'd been told to pack suggested they weren't doing it rough the whole time they'd be away. She looked across at Keaton and saw a light of determination reflected in his eyes.

"You look as though you're looking forward to this," she commented as they made their way to the exit.

He turned and flung her a brief smile. It was so fleeting she almost wondered if she'd seen it at all.

"I always enjoy tackling a new challenge," he said.

Tami felt another ripple of trepidation. "So this is going to be really testing? Like, physically?"

"Worried you're not up to it?" he said as he gestured for her to precede him on the stairs from the plane.

"Oh, I'm up to it." Then she muttered under her breath, "Even if it kills me."

She'd faced far greater challenges than those she expected to be presented by an outdoor-experience course. Like the ones she'd faced at school, where her learning style did not fit the prescribed criteria of any one of the charming boarding schools her parents had sentenced her to during her childhood. Not to mention the ones she'd faced as a child of a very privileged family, when she finally managed to get her parents to accede to sending her to the local high school in their district. A kid learned a lot about challenges in those environments. Granted, none of those required swinging from trees or navigating rapids, but there were distinct similarities.

"Good to know," Keaton said, dragging her attention back to her current situation.

Her feet touched the tarmac and she felt a surge of relief course through her to be on solid ground again. She stood back as Keaton and the pilot opened the luggage compartment of the plane and removed the packs they'd stowed earlier. The two men hefted the packs as though they weighed nothing, but Tami knew hers was around forty pounds. She probably should have packed lighter, maybe stuck to the list Keaton had given her yesterday, but a girl always needed contingencies, didn't she? And while her knitting hadn't taken up that much room, it was possible the five skeins of yarn she'd added to her bag was a little excessive.

Keaton dropped her pack at her feet. "Is there anything in there you'd like to remove before we head out? It's on the heavy side."

"No, I'm fine," Tami stubbornly insisted.

"Really, we can send anything you don't need back on the plane and they can keep it at the office for you until our return."

"I'm fine," she said adamantly.

"I won't be carrying it for you."

"I'm perfectly aware of that," she said, and to make her point she hoisted up the pack and slung one strap over her shoulder. "See? Fine."

He looked at her again and for a moment she thought he might argue, but then he firmed his lips and nodded. "Come on then. We'll go collect the car."

By the time the rental agent had shown them to the SUV he'd had ready and waiting in the parking lot, she could feel the pack beginning to rub on her shoulder. It was one thing to carry it around the house, quite another to have to lug it everywhere in a far warmer climate than back home. Maybe she should have unpacked it and left some things behind. She gave herself a mental shake. Nope. She'd made her decision and she'd stick to it. It was all part of being the new, improved Tami Wilson. And no more using the words *maybe* or *should*, either. They reeked of regret, and regret was something she didn't want in her life ever again. At least, not until she'd cleared her debt with her father.

She unslung her pack from her shoulder and shoved it firmly into the back of the SUV with a great deal of relief, then went to the passenger side of the vehicle and climbed in. She looked around at the countryside, finally allowing herself to appreciate the raw, natural beauty that surrounded them on all sides. They were atop a mesa. Below she could see the civilization that stretched before them, and all around they were bordered by the amazing rock formations and cliffs she'd so assiduously avoided looking at from the air.

"It's breathtaking, isn't it?" she said as Keaton settled in the driver's seat.

"Let's hope we both still think so when this is all over."

She wasn't sure if he was joking or not, so decided to let that one slide. Tami watched as Keaton keyed in a few details to the GPS, then she fastened her seat belt as he put the car into gear and they drove away from the airport.

"A forty-five-minute drive, you said?" she asked as they negotiated their way out of the parking lot and onto the main road, away from the airport.

"Thereabouts," Keaton responded.

"Do you mind if I put on the radio?" Tami asked, reaching for the power button on the center console.

"That will depend on the music you choose."

"I'm pretty easygoing. I listen to most things. Tell me what you like and I'll see what we can find."

"How about you find something and I'll tell you if I don't like it."

She shrugged. "Works for me."

After a few minutes she settled on a classic rock station, and as the SUV began to eat up the miles she felt the last of the tension she'd experienced on their flight ease from her muscles. She hadn't realized she'd fallen asleep until she felt Keaton shake her by the shoulder.

The woman certainly could sleep. She'd dropped off about two minutes after finding that radio station and hadn't so much as twitched since then. Still, if she was a nervous flyer, she probably was already feeling pretty tired. Add that to the early start this morning and the weight of lugging her pack around into the equation, and it was no wonder she'd dozed off.

He'd flung her the occasional glance. Just to check that she was breathing, he'd told himself, but he knew it was more than that. Knew it and didn't like it. He wasn't in the market for a girlfriend. Not now and maybe not ever. Trusting someone enough to want to spend all your free time with them was something he didn't know if he'd ever feel comfortable doing again. Logically, he knew he probably wouldn't be alone forever, but now, with the brutality of Honor's betrayal with Logan, on top of his father's web of lies, he certainly planned to be alone for a good while yet.

Keaton looked again. She wasn't conventionally beautiful. Not in the polished way the women who moved in his family's circle usually were, anyway. But Tami Wilson certainly was striking, and there was a quality to her skin that made her look almost as if there was a hidden glow from inside her. He shifted his attention back to the road ahead and growled at himself. This was not someone to stare at. She was staff and he didn't engage with staff that way. Not ever again.

By the time he pulled up at the outdoor center he was beginning to feel a little tired himself. Always an early riser, he hadn't balked at the early start today, but that, teamed with another sleepless night and driving in unfamiliar territory, made a nap look mighty promising right now. If he did naps, which he didn't. He could see his sister, Kristin, roll her eyes at the very thought of him napping. She was often telling him to slow down, to take time out, but she didn't understand how driven he was, or why.

And now, here he was, in the middle of nowhere, somewhere in Sedona, about to spend far more time with a total stranger than he'd ever anticipated. Oh, sure, he did believe in the benefits of the team-building strategy he, Logan and Kristin had all agreed upon as a strong initiative to pull their staff together again. But that was before he'd realized he'd be having his own intimate twosome for part of the trip.

"Tami, wake up. We're here," he repeated with another gentle shake of Tami's shoulder.

The woman slept like the dead.

Her eyes shot open and for a moment her pupils remained fully dilated and her gaze unfocused, but she snapped out of her daze in an instant.

"Oh, heck, I'm sorry. I didn't mean to fall asleep. That wasn't very companionable of me."

"I'm not looking for a companion," he snapped, before he could stop himself.

She looked startled for a second and then composed her features into a mask of indifference.

"Of course, you're not," she said smoothly.

In fact, it was the most professionally she'd spoken since he'd met her and he had the feeling that her instant shutdown was a facade. As if it was something she was used to doing to protect her feelings. He gave himself yet another mental shake. Why on earth was he even worried about her feelings? They were here to do a job and to learn to become a more cohesive unit…working unit, he corrected.

He alighted from the car before he could say anything else potentially volatile and extracted their packs from the back of the vehicle. Hers really was far too heavy, especially for the trekking they'd be doing in a few days' time. But she'd been adamant and he wasn't about to enter into an argument with her. *Not my circus, not my monkey*, he told himself. But she was his employee and he had a duty to her, he reminded himself. And she had a duty to him, too. They needed to build themselves into a team, and that's where his concern began and ended.

So why, then, were his eyes caught by her as she got out of the car and stretched, before bending deeply from her hips and reaching down to the red soil at her feet? And why did that fluid movement make his body tighten uncomfortably?

"Oh, it feels so good to move," she said. "I'm not used to being inactive for so long."

He cast her what he hoped was a friendly smile but he suspected more resembled a bare-toothed grimace. "I'm sure you'll have plenty of opportunity to move while we're here. We both will."

And he would need to make a note to be in front of her wherever possible. Not because he felt he was better than her. Not because he was her boss, or even because he was a natural-born leader. It had far more to do with self-preservation, because he had no doubt that if she walked ahead of him, he'd end up face-first in the red dirt of the trail because he knew he wouldn't be able to keep his eyes off that shapely butt.

Three

Keaton turned as a tall, slender man came down the stairs of the large two-story cabin, which he assumed was the accommodation block. The man stretched out his hand in welcome and a warm smile spread across his face.

"Hi, and welcome! You made good time. I'm Leon, one of your hosts and guides."

Keaton made the introductions. "Hi, I'm Keaton Richmond, and this is my assistant, Tami Wilson. The advance guard, so to speak."

Leon grinned in response. "It's a cool thing your company is doing. Come on in and I'll show you where you'll be staying until the weekend, when the others join you. It'll give you a head start on getting used to the elevation here."

"Does that mean you'll take it easy on us the first couple of days?" Tami asked.

"Perhaps a little less strenuous than what we've got planned for farther down the track," Leon said with a wink.

He turned as another man came down the stairs from the cabin. Slightly shorter than Leon and with a sturdier build, he bounded down the steps with unrepressed energy.

"Ah, here's my husband, Nathan. At the moment he's our chief cook and bottle washer until we're back to full staff for the beginning of our season. That will coincide with when the rest of your teams arrive so don't be put off by how quiet it is right now."

"Quiet is good," Tami said with a small smile. "And all too rare these days."

"I think you will enjoy it here then," Leon said before introducing Nathan to Keaton and Tami.

"Come on inside," Nathan said. "Leon will show you to your rooms and then bring you down to the kitchen. I have a late breakfast set up for you because I'm sure you're starved. You must have been up since before the birds woke today."

"It was an early start," Keaton admitted, beginning to really feel the weariness he'd tried to ignore earlier pull at him a little harder.

He stumbled a little as they picked up their packs and followed the men to the house.

"You okay?" Tami asked, a worried crease appearing between her eyebrows.

"Fine," he said shortly. "We didn't all get a nap on the way here, is all."

He didn't mean it to come out the way it did, but he saw his words found their unintentional target. Her cheeks colored up a little and she ducked her head.

"Maybe it's the altitude," she said quietly. "You don't strike me as the kind of person who suffers from a lack of sleep."

Nathan turned and looked back at them. "Don't underestimate the elevation here. We're about four thousand feet higher than what you're used to. While I don't expect you guys to suffer true altitude sickness, you may feel a little—" he paused while he searched for the right word "—hungover, for want of a better description."

"Great," Keaton muttered. "All the punishment without the fun getting there."

Leon laughed. "Oh, you'll have fun all right. Just give yourself a little time to adjust. And keep drinking plenty of water. We restock the bottles in your room fridges twice a day. Staying hydrated is probably one of the most important things you can do to cope."

After being shown to his room, Keaton took the time to have a quick shower, then returned downstairs. He followed the sounds of voices and laughter to the massive kitchen at the back of the cabin. There, Tami was perched on a barstool at one end of a large kitchen island. She looked happy and relaxed, right up until she spied Keaton standing in the doorway.

"Everything okay?" she asked. "Can I get you a coffee?"

"Fine. Everything's fine." At least it had been until he saw her again. He'd thought the time alone to get his thoughts back in line would have inured him to the ridiculous reactions he'd been having to her, but no. "And, yes, coffee would be great. Thanks."

"Black and sweet?"

He cracked a half smile. "You remembered that from yesterday?"

She shrugged. "What can I say? My mind has a cast-iron ability to remember small details."

Keaton pursed his lips and nodded. "That could definitely come in useful. As long as you never lose sight of the big picture."

Again he realized he was the direct cause of her losing the animation on her face, replacing it with that expressionless—almost subservient—look she'd worn earlier. And, dammit, he felt guilty. He needed to learn to temper his remarks. This was as much about him learning how best to work with her as it was about her working with him.

"Sorry," he said gruffly as he accepted the steaming mug of coffee she'd poured for him. "I get a bit intense at times."

"Accepted and noted," she answered with a small smile. She gestured to Nathan, who was at the wide stove. "Nathan's finishing off huevos rancheros. I keep trying to peek over his shoulder and learn his secrets, but he shooed me back to my chair. Doesn't it all smell divine?"

Keaton realized, with some relief, that he hadn't repressed her excitability completely. "It does, indeed," he agreed.

He was hungry and the food did smell great. Hungry? Hell, he was starving. Last time he'd eaten was a quick snack at the office late last night. By the time Nathan turned around with two heaping plates of steaming food, Keaton was just about drooling.

"There you go. Have at it. You'll need the energy," he said with a short laugh. "Just kidding. Leon is going to take it easy on you guys today."

"Should we be worried?" Tami asked.

"Nah, I mean it. I'm just kidding."

"I don't want to let anyone down. Especially on our first day," she said quietly.

"You'll be fine," Keaton said, feeling an uncharacteristic urge to reassure her. While this experience was supposed to test its participants, it wasn't supposed to strike fear into their hearts. "You can set the pace, okay?"

Leon arrived in the kitchen as Keaton spoke. "Sure, today's just a bit of a walk to get used to the terrain, that's all. When you've both eaten, get your hiking boots on and make sure you have day packs with a couple of bottles of water each. And wear light layers. It's going to get warmer, so you'll probably need to peel off at a certain point."

"Certainly not like the weather we left behind at home, is it?" Keaton said to Tami before sitting down beside her and tucking in to his breakfast.

"No, it's not."

While she was agreeing with him, he couldn't help but feel she had some other concerns she wasn't expressing. All in good time, he told himself. Right now he needed to apply himself to his plate. He allowed the taste explosion of the beans, eggs and salsa to fill his mouth. Beside him, Tami moaned in what was clearly an expression of extreme delight. It was an expression more suited to a bedroom than a kitchen, he mused. And just like that he felt a very unwelcome tug of desire.

Tami felt Keaton stiffen beside her. Should she have done that? She was a spontaneous person and it was only natural to her to express pleasure in something, especially something as delicious as the food on her plate. This wasn't going to be a lot of fun if she couldn't be herself. She'd spent her entire childhood being firmly reined in, and she wasn't going to permit any unnecessary restrictions in her world now, not from anyone. Keaton Richmond would just have to get used to the fact that she was open in her appreciation of the finer things in life, be they food or otherwise. And if it made him uncomfortable, then he was going to have to learn to deal with it. But thinking about her childhood and her father reminded her of why she was here in the first place, and suddenly the food in her mouth took on a bitter flavor.

She forced a smile toward their host.

"This is really good, Nathan. Thank you."

"My pleasure. Always good to see our guests enjoying our efforts."

"Are we the only ones here right now?" she asked, pushing her remaining food around her plate.

"Until the rest of your staff and those from DR Construction arrive on Saturday. Your two companies have booked us out, exclusively."

Tami looked at Keaton. "Exclusively? Wow, that's quite a commitment. To the adventure center and your staff."

Keaton shrugged. "When we do something, we like to do it right. This is all about helping all of us to work better as a team." He gestured to her now-empty plate. "Are you done? If so, we should probably get ready to go meet Leon. Remember your water."

He rose from the bench and took their plates to the deep sink on the other side of the kitchen.

She returned to her room, grabbed her day pack and stocked it with sunscreen, a light waterproof jacket in case of rain—although the sky this morning was such a clear blue she doubted it would be necessary—and three bottles of water. Tami hesitated about putting her phone in the side pocket of her bag, but remembered her father's admonition to keep it near at all times in case he needed to call or text her. She had to remember that, right now, she was operating under his instructions and, no matter how much she wanted to rebel against him, she needed to glean the information he wanted. She made sure the phone was turned to silent, then slid it in the pocket and zipped the pack closed. The last thing she wanted was to have him attempt to call her during the hike with Keaton. How on earth would she explain that? She threw on an extra layer over her long-sleeved T-shirt and jeans, laced her hiking boots and shoved her favorite hand-knitted beanie on her head, then bounded back down the stairs.

The air outside was brisk, but not quite as cool as it had been when they'd touched down at the airport earlier. The men were waiting for her as she walked outside to meet them. She groaned inwardly. She'd been quick, she knew she had, but it seemed Keaton had been quicker, and by the casual glance he made at the gold-rimmed watch on his broad wrist, he didn't like being kept waiting.

Her father had always been the same. In fact, he'd been such a stickler for time it had made her a very nervous youngster, until she'd learned that it made no difference if she was on time or not. She always disappointed him in one way or another. Even if she was on time, he wouldn't approve of what she was wearing or how she'd done her hair. After that, she'd made every effort not to be on time, knowing how much it would annoy him.

Tami sighed. She may as well grab the bull by the horns, she decided. This wasn't the time for petty games and she had a new boss to impress. And draw secrets out of, she reminded herself grimly.

"Sorry I kept you both."

"Not a problem, Tami," Leon said. "Keaton just arrived a minute or two ahead of you."

Ha! she thought with a private smirk. *So much*

for checking your watch and making me feel bad.
Instead, she merely smiled.

"Shall we go then?" she asked cheerfully.

"What's that on your head?" Keaton asked with
a bemused expression on his face.

"This?" She gestured to the glaringly bright pink
beanie. "It's so you can find me easily if I get lost.
Do you like it? I can probably knit one up for you
tonight if you want one?"

"Um, no, thank you. I don't think pink is my
color," Keaton said with a spark of humor in his
gray eyes that she found most gratifying.

It was good to bring other people joy. It was something she always strived to do and it was one of the
driving reasons why, as an adult, she'd had next to
nothing to do with her parents, who were manipu-
lative, emotional vampires at the best of times. Not
seeing them was one thing but she'd taken the further step of changing her surname from Everard to
Wilson when she turned eighteen to help increase
the emotional distance between them. Plus, it helped
her avoid the need to make excuses for not using
her family connections to give other people entry
into her father's world or, through her, access to his
money. She'd had enough of that as a kid.

"No?" she responded with a gurgle of laughter.
"I have a nice lime green that might do the trick. I
was saving it for a puppy jacket but I'm more than
happy to knit it up for you."

"A puppy jacket," Keaton said solemnly, then
raised a hand as she started to explain. "No, thank

you for the offer, but I'll be fine with my cap. Far be it from me to disadvantage an abandoned puppy." He tipped the brim of the baseball cap that was crammed over his dark blond hair and turned to Leon. "How far are we going today?"

Leon gestured to a peak that looked awfully far away to Tami's untrained eye.

"Nathan's gone on ahead on a quad bike to take our lunch supplies and extra water. We'll probably hike about an hour and a half before we get there. Maybe two hours, depending on how you're both feeling. And as to getting lost, it wouldn't be much of a team builder if we let that happen, would it? You'll be safe with us." He smiled reassuringly at Tami.

Tami wasn't sure she'd be hungry by then after the massive breakfast they'd consumed and an hour-and-a-half-to-two-hour hike seemed like an awfully long time to be traversing the terrain. Still, she was here to do a job and she needed to do it. She adjusted the straps on her day pack and hitched it onto her shoulders.

"Well, I'm as ready as I'll ever be," she said as brightly as she could.

The hike wasn't too arduous and she found it interesting to watch Keaton as he applied himself to every aspect with a quiet, calm intent. He appeared unflappable, even when a family of javelinas crossed their path partway through. For herself, the moment the odd-looking creatures that reminded her of wild boar pictures she'd seen in a *National Geographic* had appeared on the trail, she'd been ready to climb the nearest tree, but Leon had hastened to reassure her that the beasts were herbivores and were unlikely to eye her up as a potential meal. Keaton had shown interest in the creatures, but barely batted an eyelid at their long, sharp-looking, almost canine teeth that protruded from their jaws. Was he like that with everything? A lake of serenity? Or did those still waters run deep?

By the time they'd stopped and had lunch, then done the loop back to the cabin, she was beginning to wonder what her father had hoped to gain by her being with Keaton Richmond. So far they hadn't discussed work at all. In fact he appeared to be assiduously avoiding the topic. Maybe it was because Leon was with them and he was being ultracautious, but then maybe he really just wanted to stop and enjoy the scenery, too. Whichever reason, she couldn't keep bringing up work without it starting to look weird, so she opted for focusing on her breathing as they walked and enjoyed the magnificent scenery around them.

She'd grown very warm during the walk and had ended up wearing only a tank top with her jeans on the way back. A very snug tank top that hugged her body intimately.

Back at the cabin they were told they had free time to enjoy before a candlelight dinner on the enclosed deck at seven o'clock.

"Seems as though all we do here is eat," Tami remarked with a grin and a pat of her tummy.

She noted Keaton's gaze follow her movement and

focus on her stomach, then lift slowly to her breasts before tracking up to her throat and her face. A prickle of awareness made every cell in her body go to full attention. Unfortunately, that included all the cells that made up her nipples and darned if they didn't stand to attention as if it wasn't just Keaton's gaze that was on her. Her own eyes dropped to his hands. Strong, capable, long-fingered hands. Hands that right now were clenched into tight fists at his sides.

She prayed the fabric of her bra hid her reaction, but a quick glance downward confirmed her prayer had gone unanswered. Wow, like this wasn't awkward?

Tami shrugged off her day pack, with the intention of pulling out her long sleeve T-shirt and putting it back on to cover the wayward behavior of her body, but the movement made the shoulder strap of the pack catch on the straps of both her tank top and her bra, and tug them off her shoulder completely. Mortification sent heat flooding to her cheeks. Could this get any worse?

"Here, let me help you with that," Keaton said in a slightly gruff voice.

Damn, she'd annoyed him. She'd be lucky to still have a job if she kept this up, and if he sent her home she'd be out on a limb when it came to her father. Her bare skin tingled when Keaton's fingers brushed against her shoulder as he lifted the day pack off her and set it down by her feet.

"I'm not normally this clumsy," she said by way of apology. "Thanks for your help."

"No problem."

Keaton was making every effort not to make eye contact with her.

"Well, if you don't need me for anything, I'll go grab a shower and knit for a while before we meet for dinner. Okay with you?" she asked.

He gave her a curt nod. As she bent and grabbed her pack, then started up the stairs toward the house, she could feel his eyes burning on her back. She wouldn't turn around, she told herself firmly. She absolutely wouldn't. But when she got to the top of the stairs she couldn't help herself. She turned and looked at him. Keaton was still watching her, his face set into tight lines of disapproval.

She felt her stomach sink to her feet. He was regretting bringing her on this venture, she could tell. Tami gave him a small, pathetic wave, then went inside and up to her room, all the while scolding herself for giving him any opportunity to find fault with her. Under normal circumstances, his displeasure wouldn't have mattered. She'd have cut her losses and simply moved on. But she had two and a half million very important reasons to get this right and she was determined to ensure that every last dollar Pennington had stolen would be replaced in the Our People, Our Homes coffers. Then, her promise that she would make full restitution for her stupidity would be fulfilled and she could remove herself from her father's influence again. Hopefully permanently this time.

Could she really keep the promise she'd made?
She had to. There was no other choice.

Despite the directive to keep mobile-phone use
to a minimum for the duration of the team-building
exercise, Keaton couldn't resist the downtime available to him to check on the office. Kristin answered
his call on the first ring.

"Hello, brother. Missing us already?"

He could hear the teasing smile in her voice.

"Just ensuring everything is okay."

"And why wouldn't it be?" When he didn't answer, she continued. "Everything is running just as
smoothly as when you left the office last night, okay?
No one else has resigned."

"Yet."

He heard her snort of derision. "Yet," she confirmed. "How's the new assistant working out? Talk
about baptism by fire."

"What do you mean?"

"Well, you can hardly have gotten to know one
another in just one day, although it's nearly two now,
isn't it?"

"She's fine," he said succinctly.

Too damn fine, his inner voice reminded him.

"Pretty?"

"Kristin, that's unprofessional of you."

"I agree. But is she?"

Keaton rolled his eyes. His sister might be a
whiz kid with financial matters and a more-than-

competent joint-CEO, but at times she remained that annoying baby sister she'd always been.

"Pretty enough but not my type." *Liar.* "Besides, I'm not going that route again. Once bitten…"

"Keaton, I'm sorry. I shouldn't have been so asinine."

"It's okay. And, like I said, she's fine. Not what I was expecting, though."

"In what way."

"She offered to knit me a beanie."

"She what? How old is she?"

"Not sure. Although I'm guessing late twenties."

He heard his sister tapping on her keyboard. "She's thirty. And she knits beanies?"

"Puppy jackets, too. And don't say anything about her age and knitting in the same sentence or you'll be given a dressing-down on ageism."

His sister's laughter bubbled down the telephone line and filled his ear with unrepressed humor.

"She did that to you? She sounds amazing—I can't wait to meet her. You do know that knitting is a very popular pastime, for people of all ages, and that's not anything new. You could learn a thing or two from Miss Wilson. Now hang up and get back to retreating."

"It's not a retreat. It's a team-building exercise."

"Whatever, go build your team, then. For what it's worth, I'm really impressed with the enthusiasm and engagement the staff are showing with the concept. They're already beginning to discuss what strengths they can bring to the exercise and wondering which departments from DR Construction they'll be teamed with, not to mention the challenges they might have to face. This was a really good idea."

"They realize this is not a them and us situation, don't they? We're not competing with DR Construction. This is all about creating a stronger corporate bond between both companies."

"Yes, and I was talking with Lisa about the team building today," Kristin continued, mentioning their half-sister in Virginia. "All the discussion was very positive. Although apparently her mom thinks the whole thing is a waste of time and has reiterated her advice to her kids to stay well clear of us. I'm so glad Mom hasn't been like that."

Keaton grimaced. All along Eleanor Richmond, as she continued to insist on being called despite her marriage to Douglas Richmond having been proven to be void, had been a thorn in their sides. Rather than gracefully accept the truth that had been exposed about her bullying her parent's housekeeper into signing a permission for her to marry, when Eleanor was still underage, she still maintained that Douglas's intention all along had been to marry her and as far as she was concerned, that was all that mattered. Her reluctance to form any kind of bond with Douglas Richmond's other family was not mirrored by her children, thank goodness, and Fletcher, Mathias and Lisa had proven to be both professionally and personally open to the new family dynamic.

After their call ended, Keaton paced the covered deck feeling like a caged mountain cat. Kristin might see this as a good idea, but as far as he was concerned, this was shaping up to be a less-than-stellar one. Spending almost two weeks with a total stranger to build a team? It was irresponsible. He could still can the whole thing. In the face of what Kristin had said, if he pulled the plug now he'd end up doing more damage than ever. Staff were counting on this to work to rebuild the camaraderie they'd enjoyed before they'd felt their world tilt with the sudden death of Keaton's dad and the subsequent discovery of a mirror family and company on the East Coast. And not just staff, his family was counting on it, too. Which left him with only one option. To keep going.

Which meant dinner, alone with Tami tonight. He already knew their hosts wouldn't be joining them and a quick peek at the enclosed porch before he'd made his call to Kristin had shown a rather intimate setting of a table for two, together with fine silver and china, as well as flowers and candles. He forced his jaw to relax, the ache in his teeth evidence that he was clenching too tight, then, bit by bit, attempted to relax the other muscles of his body. Trouble was, there was one part of his body that seemed determined not to relax when Tami Wilson was around.

Well, it was something he'd just have to learn to deal with, he told himself. And quickly, because there were many days and nights ahead, and at the end of it, they had to have a strong working relationship because the most important thing right now was keeping Richmond Developments on an even keel.

Four

Later that evening, Keaton adjusted the collar on his suit and the knot on his tie as he checked himself one more time in the mirror. Quite a change from the outdoor gear they'd been wearing all day. Even his wind-ruffled hair was slicked back into submission and he'd trimmed his light beard to a controlled stubble. He'd wondered about the necessity to dress for dinners, but this entire exercise was about getting to understand people in all types of situations. A formal dinner party, even if it was for only two people, was a situation, after all.

He went downstairs and let himself out onto the porch. Tami had beaten him to the porch and as she turned to face him, he felt all the air leave his lungs in a giant whoosh. Dressed in a killer gown in an iridescent amethyst purple and with her hair drawn up into an updo that exposed the slender lines of her neck, she was nothing like the imp he'd caught spinning around on her office chair whom he'd met yesterday. Nor was she anything like the determined hiker who'd gamely trailed along behind him and Leon for the better part of the afternoon even when he'd sensed she was tiring. No, this vision of loveliness was another person entirely and every cell in his body responded with appreciation.

"Is something wrong?" she asked, looking hesitant. "Is this too much?"

A sackcloth and ashes would be too much.

"You look stunning."

A hint of color stained her cheeks. "I wasn't sure if it would be over-the-top, but the list you gave me did say formal dress for some meals and this is the most formal dress that I own."

"It's perfect."

Too perfect, he thought as he noted the way the fabric dipped between her breasts and skimmed the rest of her body like a second skin before elegantly flaring softly from her hips to drape at her feet. Feet that were in glittering silver sandals that added a good three inches to her height. Realizing he was staring, Keaton forced himself to walk toward the sideboard that was set up on the wall against the house. He reached for the bottle of wine that was chilling in the ice bucket. Next to it, warmed silver chafing dishes exuded delicious aromas.

"Wine?" he asked, lifting the bottle from the ice.

"Thank you, that would be nice."

Glad for something to do, he opened the wine and poured them each a small serving of the wheat-colored liquid. He passed her one of the glasses and held his up in a toast.

"To good working relationships," he said.

Inwardly, he shuddered. Man, he sounded so darn pompous. But wasn't that what this was all about? Building stronger work-based relationships?

"To working relationships," Tami murmured, then took a sip of her wine. "Mmm, that's nice. I don't usually drink chardonnay but this one is very good."

He looked at her with a little surprise. She could have seen the label and known what variety of wine it was, but he'd met few people who could tell from one sip what type they were drinking, as she'd just done.

"You know a lot about wine?"

"It was one of the few things my parents tried to educate me on that actually stuck."

"You were clearly a good student."

She snorted inelegantly, the sound in total contrast to the polished appearance of the mesmerizing creature that stood in front of him.

"I was anything but a good student." Then, as if she realized that might reflect badly on her ability to do her job, she added, "But I am very good at plenty of other things. I found, at an early age, I need to be hands-on to learn best. Theory was never one of my strong points."

Keaton found himself laughing at her self-deprecating tone. "I'm sure you have plenty of strong points to balance out your lack of application to theory."

"I like to think so. So, how about you? A good student? No, let me guess." She leaned back and studied him carefully before giving a sharp nod. "I'd say straight A's, class valedictorian and a highly competitive athlete as well. Cross-country champion— am I right?"

He nodded in amazement. "You can tell that just by looking at me?"

"Oh, I can tell a lot by looking at you," she said. "Shall we sit down?"

They sat at the small round dining table and he watched as Tami picked at her salad before she set down her fork and lifted her wineglass again.

"Well, won't you look at that. My glass is empty. Can I top you up, too?"

"Sure, but let's not go wild. Leon left me a message to say we're under our own steam for a lot of tomorrow. Some orienteering, I believe, and then an additional activity tacked on toward the end of the day. He'll meet us at that one."

She looked startled. "He's letting us out there on our own? I mean, I love the outdoors and stuff, but navigating the wild with only a map and compass sounds like it's out of my comfort zone."

"You can always wear your pink beanie in case we get lost," he teased.

"Yes, there is that," she answered with a quick smile that eased the worried line that had appeared between her brows. "Ah, well, we'll just take it all as it comes. Right?"

"Is that how you approach everything in life? Take it as it comes and see how it turns out?"

"Mostly," she acknowledged with a graceful dip of her head. "But I can make plans when absolutely necessary, too. And you? I'd wager a guess that you plan everything down to the minutest detail, and that you don't like surprises—for you, it's about the preparation and the execution, not the destination."

Again, she had him thoroughly pegged. What was she? Some kind of mind reader? Feeling a little uncomfortable at how accurate her summation of his character was, he turned his attention to the silver chafing dishes set out on the buffet against the wall. He rose from the table and went over to check what was on offer for their meal.

"You hungry?" he asked as he lifted the lid off the first one.

"I'm starving. That walk back here this afternoon burned off every last morsel we had for breakfast and lunch." She rose to join him. "Are those baby potatoes in butter and parsley sauce? My taste buds are going to think they've died and gone to heaven. What's in the next dish?"

He lifted the lid, exposing boneless chicken thighs in a rich, mushroom gravy. The unadulterated groan of anticipation that came from her next made even the hairs on the back of his neck stand to attention, along with another regrettably more visible piece of his anatomy. If she could elicit this kind of response from him just by lusting after some meat and potatoes, what would she be like when it came to more physical pleasures? Keaton slammed his thoughts closed on that question before he could get himself into serious trouble. Only a few months ago he'd been engaged to be married. His reaction to Tami had to be purely physical because he certainly didn't know her well enough to have formed any kind of connection the way he had with Honor. But then again, he'd never reacted to Honor this way, either. There'd never been that rush of arousal like he'd just experienced. And that had been exactly what had driven Honor into his brother's arms, he reminded himself.

Thankfully, Tami was busy inspecting the final chafing dish, which was divided into two sections— one with honey-and-garlic-glazed carrots, judging by the smell, and the other with steamed broccoli florets.

"This is all for us, right?" she said with a wicked gleam in her eyes.

"We are the only ones here right now."

"Then let's do it justice."

She took two plates from the warmer and began to dish up vegetables for the two of them. He took the hint and did the same with the meat and potatoes. Soon, their plates were equally laden. How on earth would she put all that away? he wondered. Actually, more to the point, how was he going to put it all away? He shouldn't have worried. It seemed he was as starving as she'd professed to be.

Keaton found himself mesmerized by the way she ate, with neatly proportioned mouthfuls on her fork being drawn to her mouth with elegant movements. From what he could tell, she applied herself to everything with care and attention to detail as well as a fair dose of enthusiasm.

When she looked up, she caught him staring. Her eyes flared slightly and a tinge of pink touched her cheeks.

"Do I have gravy on my chin?" she asked. She picked up her napkin and dabbed at her mouth.

"No, no. Sorry, I didn't realize I was staring," he said apologetically.

"Is the meal not to your liking?"

"It's great."

"Then why are you letting your food grow cold?" she said with a teasing note to her voice. "Didn't your father ever warn you not to let your meal get cold?"

"No," he said with a chuckle. "Did yours?"

Tami nodded. "And if I didn't eat every bite, he made the housekeeper serve it to me again at my next meal. One learns a certain level of compliance at an early age when faced with that."

While her words were uttered lightly, as if her childhood had been some kind of joke, she'd given him an unwitting insight into her background. Clearly discipline had been a feature in her childhood. Was that why she was so determinedly carefree now? Keaton found himself wanting to know more but schooled himself to keep his curiosity in check. Theirs was a working relationship. He didn't need to understand everything that made her who she was. He just needed her to do her job. That was all.

Once they were done, Tami pushed her plate to one side and leaned back in her chair.

"That was so good, I feel like I could climb a mountain tomorrow."

"Don't joke, we may well have to."

She leaned forward and gave him a reassuring pat on the hand.

"And if we do, we'll do it. Together, okay?"

The moment her fingertips touched him he felt a zing of electricity up his arm. *Note to self—avoid touch*, he thought. As fleeting as it was, the contact unsettled him. Maybe it was just all the stress of everything else that was going on. *Or maybe it was just Tami*, that little voice whispered.

But then his rational mind asserted itself. His reactions to Tami were an aberration. That's all it was. He was under a lot of stress with the company and with the need to rebuild trust within that company, not to mention within his own mind. He needed to cut himself some slack on his physical reaction to a woman who appealed to him. It was an instinctual response—that was all. Nothing he needed to worry about or act on. And he needed to know he could trust her. If completing this course of activities in the next few days would make that clear, it would be worth every last second of physical torture.

Wouldn't it?

Tami watched Keaton from across the table. His face, normally devoid of emotion, currently appeared to reflect a major internal battle. Today she'd discovered he was a firmly closed book when it came to sharing thoughts and feelings. Even tonight, he'd let her do most of the talking. Not that she had a problem with that—after all, jabbering on came all too naturally to her. But sometimes it was important to listen, too, and from that, to learn.

Clearly, her touch just now had unsettled him. She made a mental note to hold back on her instinctive need to physically connect with other people. She was a toucher—she hugged, she patted, she kissed. It was part of who she was, but that would have to change, especially around her new boss.

If she could hazard a guess, she'd say he'd been badly hurt somewhere along the line, and as much as she barely knew him, it made her heart ache to think that someone would close themselves off that much to the possibility of receiving warmth from another human being. She suspected that beneath the closed-door vibe Keaton gave off all the time that he was, deep down, a really nice guy. Tortured, very probably, but she suspected that he had a good heart even if he acted as if nothing really touched him deep down.

People like Keaton Richmond were a challenge and she like nothing better than to draw wounded souls to the lighter, more joyful side of life. Everyone deserved happiness, right? Well, maybe not the pond-scum-sucking douchebag who'd abused her trust and stolen the charity's money. But Keaton Richmond looked as though he carried the responsibility of the entire world on his shoulders. She wished she could have met him under other circumstances and not as a spy planted in his camp because, as things stood now, she would end up being yet another reason for him to remain cautiously shut down and that hurt. And beneath the hurt lingered a burning anger, too. If it wasn't for men like Mark Pennington and her father, people like her could simply *be*, and not be abused as tools for others' advancement. She was being forced to act contrary to everything she'd sworn to stand for and it hurt, not just on a moral level but on a deep emotional level, too. The sooner she got through this, the better.

From this point on she'd do her best to keep things businesslike. No more probing questions about him personally. Just take every opportunity to probe for information her father would find useful. Which reminded her, she needed to touch base with him tonight. He'd be expecting her call. Suddenly the meal she'd just eaten sat very heavily in her stomach.

Tami startled as she realized that Keaton was talking to her.

"I'm sorry, I was away with the fairies for a moment there," she apologized. "What did you say?"

"I was asking you if you'd like some dessert."

The last thing she wanted right now was more food, but if they didn't continue eating right now, they had very little reason to stay here at the table and talk—and she'd have less opportunity to probe him for information about Richmond Developments, too. Maybe dessert would sweeten up Keaton and encourage him to open up a little more. Maybe then she might learn something that could be useful to her father.

With her stomach groaning in protest, she answered, "I never say no to dessert."

Keaton rose from the table and cleared their plates.

"Oh, wait, let me do that!" she blurted, rising from her seat.

"It's no bother. My mom always taught us to do our share. I'll be back in a moment," he said, and disappeared through the double doors to the kitchen.

When he returned, he held two servings of tiramisu centered on plates artfully decorated with perfect balls of vanilla ice cream and shavings of chocolate. Despite her earlier reservations about consuming more food, her mouth watered at the sight of her favorite dessert.

"They really go to a lot of effort, don't they?" she commented.

She lifted her spoon and sliced into the dessert, then brought it to her mouth to taste it. She closed her eyes and moaned in delight.

"Oh, my. That's so good."

Tami looked across to Keaton, who sat frozen with an odd expression on his face.

"Are you okay?" she asked in concern. "Don't you like tiramisu?"

"I do, in fact," he said in a stilted way. "But perhaps not as much as you apparently do."

She gurgled a laugh. "Oh, the moan? I'm sorry if that unsettled you. I spent my entire childhood being forced to conform to other people's expectations. I resolved that from the moment I was responsible for myself I would embrace everything without reservation, at least once. You should try it. It's very liberating."

He stared at her for a moment before tasting his dessert.

"Mmm, very nice."

She laughed again. "Is that the best you can do?"

He tasted another spoonful and added a sliver of ice cream sprinkled with shaved chocolate, then nodded.

"It's good. What can I say?"

"Well, I guess it's a start," she conceded. "But to be honest, I wasn't just talking about trying the dessert. I meant embracing life and to heck with what others think."

He gave a derisive snort in response. "I don't have that privilege, Tami. I have a business to run and many egos to pander to."

"Does that make you happy?"

"What, pandering to other people's egos?"

She nodded.

He looked out the window for a moment, clearly formulating his answer. "I do what I have to, to get the results we need. Sometimes I even succeed. Success gives me pleasure."

She had no doubt he was playing down his level of achievement. It seemed to her that it was important to him to deliver on his promises, and that his striving for perfection drove him harder than was probably healthy. But she'd noticed he didn't answer her question.

"But does it make you happy?" she persisted.

"Of course it does." His answer was short, almost snappish, as if he didn't really like having to face the truth about whether something gave him joy or not. "Not everyone has the luxury of pursuing happiness with every breath."

Tami blinked in surprise. "You think it's a luxury?"

"Isn't it?"

"No, of course not. It's what we do anything for. It's intrinsic to our well-being."

"I think we'll have to agree to disagree on that."

"Okay," she ceded, then decided to take the bull by the horns. She'd felt her phone vibrate in her antique beaded evening bag, which she'd kept in her lap while they'd been at the table. No doubt her father was growing impatient. "How about we talk about work, then. That's why we're here, after all."

"What do you want to know?"

"Well, if we're going to work together, I think you need to open up a bit more, to be honest. I know Richmond Developments is primarily involved in construction and that you've recently begun to explore repurposing old buildings in ecofriendly ways to create microcommunities within a larger area. It sounds like a very interesting field to be involved in with the juxtaposition between old and new. Tell me more about what's coming next. What's the first project we're going to be working on together?"

Keaton played with his napkin before refolding it meticulously and placing it back on the table.

"Okay, since you're determined to discuss work, I'll do it, but I don't have to remind you about the confidentiality agreement you signed on starting with us, do I?"

Hot color flooded her cheeks. "Of course not," she spluttered, hoping he'd take it that she was insulted by his insinuation, rather than internally squirming with guilt.

She was no Mata Hari, that much was clear. To her relief, Keaton didn't seem to notice her reaction. He leaned back in his chair and began to talk, outlining a prospective contract the company was relying on to drive them through the next five years. By the sound of things, it would be huge, involving both housing and commercial interests, and for the first time it would amalgamate both arms of the businesses his father, Douglas Richmond, had established. In fact, from her research, it seemed that DR Construction and Richmond Developments had historically been rivals and she got the impression that the two families and companies merging effectively hinged on the success of winning the project.

Tami leaned forward, resting her elbows on the table, as he expanded on the plans the company had for the development.

"That sounds incredible," she enthused. "But what about low-income families? Do you have anything to offer them?"

He frowned a little. "Generally our complexes

cater to upper-middle and high-income families. It's where the money is, to be blunt. And if we develop the commercial interests around the housing complexes the right way, it's where they'll continue to spend their money, too."

"I can see the logic in that, but don't you think you have a duty of care to those who aren't as fortunate?"

"Richmond Developments, through our charitable trust, is an active supporter of several charities. Giving back to the community is something my mom has always been passionate about and it's something we take very seriously."

He looked affronted and Tami hastened to smooth the waters again.

"Yes, I'd heard that. You know my last role was with a charity and we worked in conjunction with other charities, some of which I know Richmond supports generously. But throwing money at a problem is only one aspect of solving that issue. Everyone is entitled to some pride. A lifetime of handouts is galling to a lot of people. I know—I've worked with them. Sure, there will always be those that take the easy ride, but there are more that genuinely want to get ahead, but life keeps treating them like some kind of Whack-A-Mole, keeping them in the dirt all the time. If there were better employment opportunities, childcare, low-rent accommodation and low-cost housing with low-interest finance available to more people, there'd be a chance for them to genuinely take charge of their lives and get ahead. And it's an opportunity for these families to show their kids that life's not all about hard graft and still failing."

"It's a good point, but it's not what Richmond Developments is known for."

"You've already shown you can diversify your portfolio with the renovations you're doing so successfully now. Why not become known for even more things that help build communities and pride in those communities at the same time. There are plenty of people out there who'd jump at the opportunity to work on a home that they could eventually buy for their family. You'd not only be providing homes, but job security along with a huge dose of goodwill for the firm."

"Right now we're sticking to what we know while we work to rebuild confidence in our business."

He shut her down so effectively, she knew that to belabor the point any longer would be a waste of time. But she couldn't resist one more poke at the tiger.

"Maybe it's something Richmond Developments could consider for the future?"

"Perhaps."

She looked at the half-eaten tiramisu on her plate. She really couldn't force down another bite, as delicious as it had been. An unexpected yawn caught her unawares and she covered her mouth with her hand.

"I'm sorry," she apologized. "It seems as if I've hit my limit for today. If you don't mind, I think I'll head up to bed."

"No problem. We have an early start and a full day tomorrow. I'll be heading up shortly, too."

She rose from the table and clutched the beaded bag in her hand. It vibrated again, letting her know she hadn't yet responded to however many messages had been left on there.

"Okay then, I'll see you tomorrow morning at breakfast. Six?" she asked.

He inclined his head slightly in acknowledgement and turned his attention to the darkness outside. Tami turned and walked away. She stopped at the door and hesitated. Looked back. He was still in the same position, and in that brief unguarded moment he looked so very lonely. So isolated. It made her heart ache. Every nerve in her body screamed at her to stop and go back, but her brain very firmly instructed her that would not be a good idea. He wasn't ready to let down his defenses and he wouldn't welcome her probing behind them. That much was very clear.

Five

"No! I won't do it."

Tami was emphatic and on the verge of tears, something that made Keaton feel intensely uncomfortable. He didn't do tears. Not his mom's, not his sister's, not anyone's. Tears were a reflection of unbridled emotion and that made him squirm.

"Come on, it's perfectly safe," he coaxed.

She shook her head, crossed her arms and took several steps away from the platform erected at the edge of the sandstone outcrop.

"No."

"You came on the plane," Keaton reasoned. "We flew far higher than this."

"With metal tubing all around us, and engines propelling us forward and we had seat belts and a pilot. This," she said, flinging her arm out toward the zip line that extended from their location to some point in the distance they could barely see in the foliage on the other side of the canyon. "This is sheer madness."

Keaton looked at her. She was genuinely frightened. No, judging by the fresh perspiration that soaked the armpits of her T-shirt and her rapid breathing, *terrified* was probably a better word for it. To be honest, he was surprised. She'd been so intrepid on their hike to get to this point on the cliffside. Her interpretation of the instructions had occasionally been a little offbeat, but they'd made it to their destination in good time and, on the way, it had been an interesting insight into how her mind worked. He felt his lips twist into a rueful smile. Worked? Bounced around like a high-density rubber ball, more like.

His first impression of her in the office a couple of days ago had not been a great one. Seeing her spinning on her office chair with reckless abandon had felt like an affront to him, an indication that she wasn't prepared to take her role as his executive assistant seriously. But the past couple of days had shown him that she wasn't quite the flighty character she appeared to be on the surface, and her deep compassion for those less fortunate—something she'd volubly demonstrated last night—exhibited a clear understanding of their plight.

He hadn't been able to stop thinking about it after she'd gone up to her room, and he'd emailed Kristin and Logan to ask if they could look in to the logistics and viability of including some lower-cost housing into their plan. It was only after he'd done that that he'd been able to drift off to sleep somewhere around midnight.

But right now, his biggest challenge was getting Tami on that zip line, and her adamant refusal to even step into the harness was something he hadn't anticipated.

"There's lunch at the other side," he said in an attempt to cajole her.

"I figure if I climb back down and start walking it'll only take me another hour. I can wait that long."

Her stomach rumbled loudly.

"Or we can be there in a couple of minutes."

Her stomach rumbled again.

Keaton tried again. "C'mon, I've seen little kids do this with their parents. How bad can it be?"

"Have you seen how high we are? Do you understand anything about terminal velocity and the laws of physics?"

Keaton couldn't help it. He laughed. In fact, he laughed so hard, he felt tears spring to his eyes.

"Actually, yeah, I do. Physics was one of my better subjects at school."

"Of course it was," she muttered and turned away from him in disgust.

"Tami, please—trust me. You'll be completely safe. How about this—why don't we go in tandem? Would that make it easier for you?"

She turned back to face him, her lower lip caught between her teeth and a nervous expression on her face.

"We could do that?"

Keaton looked across to Leon, who had met them here at the zip line launch point and who was waiting patiently to harness them up. He must have seen this kind of reaction many times before, Keaton realized, because he made no move to rush them along. The fact they were the only ones there probably helped, too.

"Leon? Would we be able to go across in tandem?" Keaton asked.

"Sure," Leon answered. "Just give me a few minutes to change the rigging."

Tami's eyes were wide when Keaton looked at her.

"There, see? Problem solved."

"I think you're forgetting one thing," Tami insisted.

"What's that?"

"Me. I can't do it. I. Just. Can't."

"Of course you can. Look, you conquered your fear of flying. This is way more fun. And like I said before—lunch."

"Flying took me years, Keaton. Years!"

"Well, we don't have years. We have now. C'mon. Where's your adventurous spirit. I know I don't know you all that well yet, but you strike me as the kind of woman who usually gives anything a go, right? And didn't you tell me last night that you'll try anything once?" he paraphrased in reminder.

She begrudgingly nodded.

"Then let's do this."

She sighed heavily, then uncrossed her arms.

"Okay. But if I throw up all over you, it'll be your own fault."

Keaton fought the urge to fist-pump the air in triumph, but reminded himself quickly that they weren't there yet. And then there was the vomit thing. He really didn't want that to happen. He held out his hand.

"Look, I'm with you every step of the way. I trusted you to get us here during the orientation and you can trust me to keep you safe on the zip line. Okay? Let's go get harnessed up."

She tentatively accepted his hand, her smaller fingers curling around his and sending a trickle of warmth up his arm. Trust. It was such a simple concept, yet the weight of it was huge. He could feel the tremors that rocked her body as they walked toward Leon, but she didn't balk. He honestly hadn't considered what pushing her to do this might cost her in emotional terms until he held her hand right now. The sense of responsibility that put on his shoulders was huge.

"All ready?" Leon asked, looking carefully at them both.

"We are," Keaton said firmly. "In tandem, okay?"

"Yep, I've got the harnesses all set. Tami? Are you sure you're okay with this?" Leon asked her directly.

She nodded. "Let's just get it over with."

Leon moved quickly and efficiently to get them into their harnesses and gave them simple instructions on what to do and what to expect when they reached the other side. They positioned themselves at the end of the platform and Tami emitted a small moan that was as different from her delight in good food as chalk was from cheese. She was absolutely terrified—he could feel it in every quake of her body.

"Any last requests?" Leon said cheerfully as he smiled from his position at the other end of the platform.

Keaton laughed and looked down at Tami. Her arms were wrapped firmly around him and her eyes were scrunched shut. And were those tears squeezing out from under her lashes?

"We can do this. C'mon, Tami," he said firmly. "We'll go on three, okay? One, two, three!"

And then they were flying. Tami's eyes sprung open the second they launched, but she didn't so much as scream or say a word. In fact, Keaton wasn't even certain she was breathing. He was so busy watching her, he hardly noticed the journey himself, and it was over all too quickly. Nathan was waiting on the landing platform at the other side.

"So, guys, how was it?" he asked with a beaming smile on his broad face.

Keaton looked at Tami, who was as white as a ghost. Would she need medical attention? he wondered worriedly. But then a transformation took place and a massive grin pulled her lips wide. Excited energy poured off her in waves and she danced a little jig as she shrugged out of her harness. Tami looked back along the zip line they'd traveled on before turning toward him and Nathan.

She closed the short distance between them and grabbed his hand, then reached up and planted a kiss on his lips.

"That was a-mazing! Thank you so much for making me do it. Can we do it again?"

Keaton looked at her in absolute shock, his lips tingling from the unexpected contact. His face must have reflected his surprise because the joy in her eyes dimmed instantly and she took several steps back.

"Oh, heck, I'm sorry. I overstepped the mark, didn't I? That was really inappropriate."

"It's okay," he said stiffly. "I'm glad you enjoyed it in the end."

"And you? Did you enjoy it, too?"

"I think I was too concerned for your safety and state of mind to even be aware of what was happening, to be honest."

She gave him a smile. "Thank you. I really mean it. Without your support, I would never have attempted anything like that. I guess that's a tick in the box for teamwork, right?"

He barked a short laugh. "Yeah, that's a tick in the box, all right."

While they'd been talking, Nathan gathered up all their equipment and packed it away. When he was done, he joined them and asked them to follow him to a lookout, where they'd be enjoying lunch. The whole way there, Keaton tried not to think about that kiss. It had been spontaneous. Something born of her sheer joy in conquering a fear. He compressed his lips more firmly together in an attempt to rid himself of the memory of the soft, sweet pressure of her mouth on his.

It had meant nothing, right?

Right. It couldn't mean anything. He wouldn't let it. These were extreme circumstances and they'd just taken part in an extreme event together. Emotions, especially hers, had been running high. There. He'd managed to compartmentalize it. Fold it neatly in a box and shove it into the darker recesses of his mind. Where it would stay. And he wouldn't think about how it had felt to have her arms tightly wound around his body as they'd swung along the zip line, or how her hands had clung to him as if he was the only thing between her and certain death. Nope, not at all.

Tami stood outside in the cool morning air and watched the sun begin to rise. Her fingers were wrapped around a hot, steaming mug of coffee and she listened to the sounds of the desert waking around her. The past few days had been a challenge. Not physically—at least, not too much—because with each day she felt stronger and fitter and more capable of the tasks that had been set before them. But mentally things had been tough. She'd let her exuberance cross personal boundaries after the zip line and that was not a good thing. Keaton had been very distant with her since then. Sure, they'd enjoyed their dinners together, and by mutual agreement had continued to discuss work over the table, but there'd been nothing personal. In its own way that was a relief. Tami wasn't about to race to reveal her own past, but she couldn't help being more curious about Keaton's. It was one thing to probe his plans for Richmond Developments, moving forward, and he was opening up more and more about that, but her dad had made it clear in last night's text message that he wanted all the information she could get on the family members themselves. It turned her stomach to think her father would use the information she passed him against the Richmonds but, as he had reminded her again last night, she was here to do a job—for him and no one else.

At least they wouldn't be forced to spend as much time alone together from today. Two new groups would join them today, one headed by Fletcher Richmond, from Virginia. Apparently, he was the eldest Richmond brother and from the secret family Keaton's dad had maintained on the East Coast. The other group was headed by Logan Parker-Richmond, the long-lost twin. She'd met him, and his fiancée, Honor Gould, very briefly on her first day with Richmond Developments. She'd been struck by just how identical the twins were. But where Keaton had a simmering intensity and a very driven attitude, Logan appeared to be a little less intimidating. Maybe it was because when he'd found his family, he'd also been lucky enough to find love with Honor at the same time. Or maybe it was just the way he'd been raised.

Tami remembered hearing a little about his situation and how he'd been abducted from the hospital nursery as a newborn and then spirited away to New Zealand, where he'd been brought up by his abductor and her family. From what she'd heard and seen of New Zealand in the media and from friends who'd visited the country, the lifestyle there was relaxed and less frenetic than many other parts of the world and the few Kiwis she'd met had an easygoing way about them. Even in that brief introduction she had to him, Logan certainly appeared to be more laid-back than Keaton. It would be interesting to see how the two brothers interacted together.

What she had noticed even in her brief stint in the office on her first day, was a distance between Logan's fiancée and Keaton. She wondered if there was something to that or if she'd just imagined things. Obviously things were strained in the office with all the turmoil they'd been through, and with Tami being the newbie on the floor, it wasn't as if she'd been privy to the details of what had been going on prior to her starting there.

Ah, well, she told herself. The next few days with the new teams would give her plenty of time to get to know others better. And to hopefully find something to get her father off her back. She'd tried ignoring his text messages but that had only encouraged him to try phoning her, which had not been at all convenient. In the end, she'd told him she'd check in, by text, each night. Though she'd taken notes on her phone each day after dinner, she didn't really share the details, only sending her dad the briefest of messages before she went to bed. If he wanted more than that, he would just have to wait until she returned to Seattle and made her full report.

And while making that statement clearly in her head should have made her feel as though she was in control, she'd never felt less so in her life. Over her head still hung the obligation she had to somehow repay the money Mark had stolen. She'd given her word she would, and it was only on that promise that the administrators at Our People, Our Homes had agreed not to go to the police…yet. The whole thing made her stomach crunch in a tight knot. She sighed heavily.

"Everything okay?"

She spun around as Keaton came across to join her.

"Yes, sure."

"You just looked as if something was bothering you. Or maybe it's just that you're supposedly not your best until eight a.m.," he said with an injection of levity.

The man was too astute for his own good. Tami forced a smile to her face. There'd be distraction enough to keep her mind off things very soon.

"No, I'm fine. Kind of wondering how we're all going to work together when the new teams arrive, I guess."

"Well, in the initial couple of days we'll each be pairing up with someone from Virginia. DR Construction run on very similar lines to us and have experienced similar fallout from my father's deceit." His mouth twisted harshly on that last word. "Anyway, we're all committed to making this work, going forward. The sooner we get used to each other, the more easily we'll work together. After breakfast, let's go through those pairing lists before everyone else begins to arrive."

"Yes, good idea. I see Leon and Nathan's extra staff have begun to arrive, too."

Keaton looked back at the main cabin and surrounding buildings, which were starting to light up with new activity. "Yeah, it's going to feel quite different, but I'm glad we had this time to work out the kinks ahead of time."

"Not that there really were any," she commented.

"True. The guys run a well-oiled machine here." He went over to the coffee carafe on the hot plate and poured himself a mugful. "Shall we go in for breakfast?"

"In a minute. I just wanted to watch the sunrise. It's something I don't take time to do at home."

He stood beside her in the stillness as they faced east and watched the myriad shades of gold and orange as they unfurled into the sky. There was a calmness that came from being alone with Keaton that she'd never experienced with anyone else. Despite what he'd said when she'd started at Richmond— about speaking without thinking—she'd noticed he was happy to be silent, which was something she never did enough of. After a few more minutes of watching the sky, she tipped the last of her coffee into the bushes and turned to the cabin.

"I guess we'd better go in and start preparing for the day," she said stoically.

"You don't sound keen. Is there a problem I need to know about?"

"No—no problem. I've just enjoyed it being just us here. More than I thought I would, to be honest. It's going to feel strange being surrounded by a whole lot more people again, even if it is the purposes of the whole exercise."

"Yeah," he said with a slow smile. "I get what you mean. But we'll adjust. C'mon. Let's go eat."

After breakfast, Keaton got up and helped himself to more coffee from the perpetually brewing pot on the countertop.

"More for you, too?" he asked.

"Any more and I'll be jittering, so, no thank you. I guess I'd better go and get ready. I have the printed name lists in my pack. I'll bring them down in a few minutes."

She got down from her stool and headed for the door.

"Good, thanks. Oh, and Tami?"

She hesitated and faced him. "Yes?"

"I just wanted to say I've been really impressed by how you've tackled the challenges we've been set. I think we're going to work really well together when we get home."

"Was there ever any doubt?" she asked flippantly.

"Well, including spinning around on office furniture, you've managed to surprise me every day with your strength and resilience."

"A girl's gotta do what a girl's gotta do," she said, suddenly feeling awkward.

He cracked a grin that just about made her knees

melt. "Yeah, something like that. Anyway, I just wanted to say that I'm really glad you're on my team."

"Me, too."

She would have said more but her throat had choked up on the swell of guilt that pummeled through her with the pace of a freight train. On his team? She hadn't been on his team from the minute she'd set foot inside Richmond Developments. He was beginning to trust her, which was exactly what she'd needed, but she was going to take that carefully wrought trust and exploit it. Use it against him in the cruelest way imaginable. Remembering that fact made her feel sick in her soul. She liked Keaton. Was attracted to him, too, to be totally honest. Knowing that she was merely a tool of her father's making—being used to bring Richmond Developments down another notch—made her the worst kind of person and totally undeserving of Keaton's praise. But she couldn't tell him any of that, could she?

Tami swiftly turned and went back upstairs to her room. Once there, she locked her door behind her and took out her phone. Yes, there was another message from her father.

Remember your promise to me.

She blew out a breath and composed a text reply.

Going off grid for a couple of days. Will text on return.

She pressed Send and waited for his reply. She didn't have to wait long.

You'd better have something good for me by then.

His disapproval was loud and clear. Tami checked the phone was fully charged and turned off all mobile data before tucking it away in her pack. Not for the first time she wished she'd been born into a different family. Even a family like the Richmonds, who'd had their fair share of trouble, but still remained tightly knit despite everything.

She couldn't remember a single time her father had told her he loved her, or was even proud of her. And for as long as Tami could recall, her mother had made it clear that she needed to conform if she wanted to be loved. She'd tried—oh, how she'd tried. But conformity had never been her style and never would be. She was the child, at junior ballet, who happily skipped in the opposite direction to everyone else—the one at gymnastics who preferred wildly executed somersaults on the mat to carefully per-formed balance-beam routines. As far as her fam-ily was concerned, she was a rough, square peg in a smoothly round and highly polished hole. But whether she liked it or not, they were the only route out of her current predicament.

A wave of rage against Mark Pennington and his deceit and greed poured through her. She breathed her way through it, allowing it to fill every nook and cranny of her mind before letting it, and all the tension that gripped her body with his memory, go. She'd permitted him to woo her—welcomed it, in fact. But, just like every other bad decision she'd made in her life when it came to men, she'd been blind to his faults and all too trusting. How ironic, she thought, as she went to the bathroom to finish getting ready for the day, that she should now be on the other side of the coin. She was the one who shouldn't be trusted right now. She was the danger. And she'd never been more miserable about anything in her life.

Keaton's words downstairs had rammed it all home to her. When it was discovered that she was a deliberately planted mole, and she had no doubt it would come out one day, he'd hate her. And that prospect made her hurt to her core. Not so much because she'd have breached her employment agreement and the confidentiality clauses she'd signed with the fingers of one hand crossed behind her back, but for the fact that she'd won Keaton's trust and would stomp it into the ground like sand before this was all over. But she had two and a half million reasons to see this through. More than that, she had the expectations and the needs of every beneficiary of Our People, Our Homes weighing on her shoulders at the same time.

Tami blew out one more breath and, after grabbing the team lists, headed back downstairs. Time to face the day.

Six

Keaton watched as everyone hoisted their packs and prepared for the hike toward the river. So far everything seemed to be going well, although he still found it hard to accept Fletcher Richmond was his half brother. Seemed there was barely a moment when there wasn't another sibling popping out of the woodwork, he thought with a large dose of cynicism.

Logan was on the other side of the group, Honor never far from his side. He'd caught a sideways glance from her earlier, not long after their arrival, and felt a twinge of something he really didn't care to examine too carefully. Was it envy? Granted, Honor had mistaken Logan, his identical twin, for him and had thought she was sleeping with Keaton that night before Christmas last year. It rapidly became obvious that the two of them were inexplicably drawn to one another and as far as he and Honor were concerned, on a personal level at the least, the writing had been on the wall.

He'd been the one to end their engagement. What else could a man do when he'd been cuckolded by his own twin? But it hadn't taken long for him to realize that he wasn't heartbroken by the event. Angry, yes. Cheated, definitely. But when push came to shove, his disappointment in Honor's betrayal had been just that. Disappointment. Not heartrending sorrow. Not vengeance-seeking fury. It was galling to admit to himself that the woman he'd planned to spend the rest of his life with really didn't matter as much to him on an emotional level as he'd once believed. It didn't make seeing her with Logan comfortable just yet, but in time that would come. It had to. He would not be responsible for creating any further divisions in a family already torn apart by his father's actions.

He shifted his gaze to where Tami was completing her duty of letting everyone know whom they'd be pairing with. At least he could rely on her. It was a rare feeling to know he could depend on someone, especially after these past three months.

"Okay, everyone," Keaton called out. "Follow Tami and our guide, Leon, down to the river and he'll allocate us to our two-man inflatable kayaks. Nathan and I will bring up the rear. If anyone has any problems or issues on the hike, we all stop. Is that clear?"

After a cavalcade of assents, Keaton nodded to

Tami and Leon to lead off on the trail. During the hike, he heard more than a few grumbles, but it wasn't long before everyone settled into a steady stride and appeared to be enjoying the clean air and crisp, clear weather. Once they were by the river, Fletcher came up alongside him. He wouldn't have been his first choice of partner in this exercise. For all that he barely knew his half brother, he'd have preferred someone he didn't know at all, but then again maybe this would help cement a better relationship between them.

"This exercise was a good idea. Not exactly comfortable, but a good idea nonetheless," Fletcher said with a grin that reminded Keaton all too much of their father.

"Thanks, but it wasn't just mine. We all worked on it."

"But you undertook the logistics of putting it in place. It'll be interesting to see how everyone mixes together. Nice new assistant, by the way. She seems capable."

"Yeah, she is."

"You two seem to work well together."

"It would have made this difficult if we didn't. Did you have much pushback from any of your staff about the venture?"

Fletcher grimaced. "A few of the older staff in senior management—Dad's die-hards. Not so keen to step out of their comfort zones, especially with who they still see as the opposition, y'know?"

"Yeah, I know. It was the same for us," Keaton

said with a grin at his half brother. "Not that we have many die-hards left, to be honest."

"Same. Dad's actions betrayed a lot more people than just his immediate family. But we'll get through it. And we'll be stronger for it, too," Fletcher said emphatically.

In that moment, Keaton felt an odd sense of kinship with his half brother. Something he hadn't anticipated, given the way their two families had been drawn together. Meeting for the first time over the grave of their dead father hadn't made the familial connection a sweet one, he reminded himself sardonically. Maybe things would be better all-around after this exercise.

At the river, everyone assembled in their pairs, and amid much laughter and a few squeals and much rocking of the kayaks, they all went on the river. Their packs were loaded into small trailers that were being towed by ATVs by some of Leon and Nathan's additional staff to the campsite farther downstream. Keaton found Tami in the group and watched her carefully as she paddled with her partner well ahead of him and Fletcher.

"She's doing okay," Fletcher said from behind him.

"Who?"

"Your assistant, Tami."

"What makes you think I'm keeping an eye on her?" Keaton said defensively.

"Man, you can barely look anywhere else."

Had he really been that focused on her? "I'm just keeping tabs on all my staff. Aren't you?"

"Yeah, sure."

But Keaton could hear the faint humor threaded through his half brother's response and decided to make a concerted effort not to keep watching out for Tami.

In all, they spent just over an hour on the river. Several areas were low-grade white water, and required more concentration than others, but overall the journey was quite serene. Keaton realized that this was the first time he'd actually begun to relax and unwind in many months. And he and Fletcher worked well together on the water, their strokes even and well-matched. Better still, Fletcher didn't seem to feel the need to fill the relative quiet with inane chatter. Maybe he and his half brother were more alike than he'd ever considered.

By the time they made it to the campsite, there were a few complaints about blisters and sore butts from sitting in one position so long, but overall the mood was buoyant. Everyone began erecting their sleeping quarters for the night, still in their matched pairs. Tami and her partner appeared to be struggling a little, not having pegged the base of the tent down first, but amid much laughter they eventually got there and were the last to complete their setup. He found it fascinating watching her. She appeared to be able to find common ground with everyone she spoke to and did so effortlessly. He envied her that talent.

"Still watching her, bro," Fletcher said quietly from behind him. "But I can see why. She's quite the package."

Keaton wheeled around. "If I'm watching her it's only out of concern, not anything else. I've been down the route of an office-based relationship before. I'm not heading on that road again. Intimacy does not belong in the workplace."

"Noted." Fletcher rubbed his chin with one hand, looking speculatively in Tami's direction. "Do you think long-distance would work?"

"No, I don't," Keaton said before he realized the other man had deliberately baited him. "And stay away from my assistant."

Fletcher laughed as he walked away and Keaton felt his lips twitch into a smile.

Over the next six days the groups completed high-ropes courses and a mountain bike trek, and spent a day rock climbing—the latter affording them incredible views across the heart-stoppingly beautiful vista of towering red-rock towers and cliffs amid more hiking and another stretch of kayaking on the river. Keaton felt renewed and invigorated by the time they started the hike back to the cabins. He and Fletcher had forged a much stronger friendship during their team challenges against other small groups, and for the first time in what felt like forever, Keaton was looking forward to what the future brought.

Tami, however, appeared to become more tense with each day. He'd wondered if it was all the aerial work they'd had to do, but she'd applied herself to everything with far more enthusiasm than she had the zip-lining. But something was clearly bothering her. Maybe he'd be able to coax it out of her tonight, after the dinner and party they were going to have in celebration of the end of the exercise. And then again, he reminded himself, maybe it was none of his business.

Leon and Nathan and their staff had coordinated a spectacular meal and festivities, with their own special set of awards for people they'd thought had come the furthest in terms of development, both personal and as groups of two or more. Keaton was pleased to see one of the older members of Fletcher's team win an award. The guy had really come out of his shell, transforming from an impatient and reluctant piece of work to someone who'd shown compassion and leadership in a group challenge the day they'd had to find a way to bridge a fast-moving section of water. And then there was Logan and Honor. Keaton had had little to do with them during most of the challenges, but he was pleased to see them given a commendation for the way they'd not only worked together when pitted in direct opposition to one another, but also how they'd encouraged their teams.

Overall, everyone appeared to have had a great time and it was interesting to see both sides of Richmond Developments and DR Construction mingling freely. On the surface, the exercise had achieved the sense of camaraderie Keaton knew they'd need moving forward. There was only one fly in the ointment. Tami. She still had an air of distraction around her and her smiles were few and far between. Something was definitely bothering her.

Tonight she was dressed again in the stunning purple gown she'd worn on their first night here, and Keaton wasn't oblivious to the admiring glances that were sent her way by many of the people gathered there. He wanted to tell them all not to look at her that way, that she wasn't a piece of meat to be hungered after, but then drew himself up short. What was it to him, anyway? Maybe she'd be happy for the attention. Besides, it wasn't as if he had any kind of claim on her.

By the time the evening wound down, with everyone exhausted and heading off to their allocated cabins and beds before the early start back home in the morning, Keaton decided now was the time to check on Tami's mood. She'd been going from table to table, ensuring no one had left anything behind. She hadn't seen him approach her and he saw her flinch a little when she realized he was standing right there beside her.

"Everything okay?" she asked. "I didn't forget anything, did I?"

Keaton shook his head. "No, everything went perfectly. In fact, with you only having started with us the day before we embarked on this thing, you were exemplary with how you hit the ground running. I'm glad you were here, Tami."

A small smile pulled at her lips. He'd expected her reaction to his praise to be more enthusiastic, but perhaps she was just tired, too.

"Thank you," she said softly. "Was there anything else?"

He was about to tell her to go on up to her room, but that worry about her demeanor prodded him again.

"You don't seem to be yourself, tonight," he said. "Is something wrong?"

Tami looked at him in shock. She'd thought she'd hid it well, but then again, given the type of man she'd discovered Keaton to be, maybe it wasn't such a surprise that he could read her better than everyone else.

"I guess I'm just wondering how I'm going to do once we're away from here and back in the office," she hedged.

It was a poor excuse for an explanation, but she could hardly tell him that she was terrified by the fast-approaching deadline that awaited her. She forced herself to smile.

"I know," she continued, "it's silly, right?"

"Yeah, it's silly. You'll be fine. *We'll* be fine."

"I've enjoyed the time here. It's made me realize I can do so much more than I'd ever believed I could do."

Keaton nodded. "I know what you mean. It's been an eye-opener."

She heard him sigh a little and followed his line of sight. Outside the dining room, Logan and Honor walked arm in arm toward their cabin. Seeing the two of them so engrossed in one another made Tami's heart ache for Keaton. From a conversation with another Richmond Developments staffer, Tami had heard that Honor had been previously engaged to Keaton until his twin came out of the woodwork. She'd noticed that Keaton had had very little to do with the couple during their camping trip and that his interactions with Logan had been stilted. Did Keaton still harbor feelings for Honor? It couldn't be easy to see the woman you loved transfer her affections to your mirror image.

Tami took a step closer to Keaton and put a hand on his shoulder. She wanted to draw his attention away from something that was a very painful reminder. It made sense that Keaton would keep himself shielded from emotional harm, and Tami's nature made her want to protect him from that, too. Her nature? she asked herself. No, she had to be honest. She was becoming more and more attracted to her boss. An unfortunate truth, when she forced herself to look at it under a microscope, because wasn't that exactly what had gotten her into the financial trouble she was now in? But Keaton was nothing like Mark. He was honorable and true. He'd never abuse another's trust and then cut and run, leaving someone he'd professed to love to face the music all alone, not to mention setting them up to look complicit in the bargain.

Keaton reacted to her touch and turned to her with a face that could have been carved from granite.

"Keaton?"

She watched as his eyes focused on her and as the cold expression that had been there a moment ago dissolved into something else. His pupils flared and she heard the slight hitch in his breath before he reached for her and dipped his head to take her lips in a kiss that seared away any thought of anything or anyone else.

Heat blossomed through her body, coalescing deep inside her as his mouth teased hers open and his tongue swept her own. She felt her knees grow weak and she clung to him with both hands as he angled his head and deepened their kiss. He tasted of something sinfully, delightfully decadent. It took her a second to realize that it was purely him, and she wanted more. She kissed him back, tasting him as he tasted her, her fingers stroking the back of his neck. His strong hands pulled her even closer and she felt the hard evidence of his arousal against her lower belly. The embers at her core flamed higher as she shifted against him, first one way, then the other.

She wanted to feel him everywhere—she wanted to learn every inch of him in return. Just then, a clatter of pots from behind the kitchen door at the far end of the dining room echoed through the space around them. They sprang apart, creating a yawning distance between one another that left her feeling bereft until she realized she'd just been kissing her boss.

"I—" she began, but Keaton put a hand up to stop her.

"No. Don't apologize. Don't say a word. The fault here was entirely mine. I overstepped my position as your employer and I took advantage of you when you were obviously in need of support. That was wrong of me. It won't happen again."

"Keaton, I—"

She tried to speak but he simply acted as if she'd said nothing.

"Obviously, if my actions have left you uncomfortable about continuing to work with me, I won't hold it against you. I can find you another position within the company or make sure you receive the appropriate assistance until you find another role somewhere else."

What? What was he saying? Did he want her out of Richmond Developments? No! She couldn't let that happen. And who was this stranger standing in front of her now, anyway? He was nothing like the man who'd drawn her into his arms and kissed her just now as if their very existence depended on it. Tami's entire body hummed with suppressed energy, burned with molten desire. With sheer need for him. She took a step forward, but hesitated as his eyes once again grew cold and distant. His breathing might be a little faster than normal, but he'd managed to get himself back under control a whole lot quicker than someone who'd genuinely been invested in what they'd just shared.

Had she been a convenient outlet for his frustration over his doomed relationship with Honor? Was that all it had been? She dragged her scattered wits together and pushed away the hurt that now lodged deep in her chest.

"No need to apologize. It was nothing," she said with all the dignity she could muster. "We've had a challenging time and we needed an outlet. Don't worry, I don't hold you responsible for something we both clearly wanted at the time. And, please, don't worry that it will cause a problem for us at work. I'm sure we can get along just fine without hashing this out any further."

"Tami, I—"

"Good night, Keaton," she said firmly.

She deliberately turned her back and paused by her table, then collected her evening bag and exited the room. She held herself together through the dining room, out the door and up the stairs, but the moment her door was closed and locked behind her, she lost it. Her entire body shook as tremors took her over and the tears that she'd so staunchly kept in check until she was alone began to track down her cheeks.

She'd done it again. She'd fallen for someone who didn't want to love her. Was she so desperate for affection that she'd just accept whatever emotional bone was thrown in her direction? No, she deserved better. And Keaton, too—he deserved to know that life wasn't always about rigid control. Sadly, she accepted she wouldn't be the one to show him that.

Seven

The flight home was quite different from the one to Sedona. Every seat on the private jet was taken and other Seattle-based staff had boarded a charter aircraft that was leaving just after the Richmond jet took off. The Virginia-based group were heading back on another charter flight shortly after. There was a hum of conversation around them that filled the awkward silence that persisted between Tami and Keaton.

Tami had barely slept a wink last night and, judging by the look of him, Keaton hadn't, either. Logan and Honor were on the flight with them, seated opposite, and she couldn't help but notice the number of times Keaton glanced at them both, then looked away equally quickly. More and more she wondered if Keaton was still in love with Honor. It had to be tough, working with the woman you were going to marry and watching a man who was a virtual stranger to you, and yet your mirror image at the same time, sweep her out right from under you.

Poor Keaton—he'd been through so much. She could understand why he wouldn't want to pursue another office-based relationship. She didn't, either, as her last liaison had turned into a complete disaster, too. A disaster that had planted her firmly in the Richmond family's path, where she was supposed to be the instrument of their next failure. The whole idea twisted her stomach in knots. Hadn't the Richmond family all been through enough already?

She didn't want to be the one responsible for making Keaton's life even more difficult than it had been in the past three months, but she was committed to doing so if she was going to get out of the hellhole Mark had left her in. And her dad would only keep his end of the bargain if she gave him a scoop on whatever Richmond Developments was planning. And until she'd gone through all her notes, she wasn't even sure she'd have anything he'd consider important enough. The very idea that she'd have to betray Keaton, the entire company and all its employees— many of whom she'd now struck up firm friendships with over the course of the trip—it all made her stomach pitch and heave. She swallowed hard.

"Tami? Are you feeling okay? You've gone very pale," Honor asked from where she sat across from Tami.

"I'll be fine."

Honor summoned a cabin-crew member and requested some sparkling water for Tami to sip on. She
also reached into her bag and passed Tami a small
packet of crystalized ginger.

"Chew on one of those. It'll help with your stomach."

Tami smiled gratefully at Honor's consideration,
but she seriously doubted that a cube of ginger and
some fresh water would fix what ailed her. Either
way, she did as she was told and then sought refuge
in sleep for the balance of the journey. It was only
when a strong male hand clamped on her shoulder
and gave her a little shake that she realized she'd slid
across in her chair and was snuggled up against Keaton. She moved back instantly.

"I'm so sorry, I didn't know I'd—" she spluttered.

"It's okay. Don't fuss. We're preparing to land."

His voice was brusque, his words clipped. Of all
the stupid things she could have done, sleeping on
top of him was nearing the top of the list. Of course,
kissing him after the zip line ranked right up there at
the very top, alongside kissing him back like a wan-
ton woman, as she had last night. And while Keaton's
unbridled passion had taken her by surprise, she'd
loved every second of it. Clearly, he did not feel the
same way, and she had to accept that. Maybe she'd
just been a convenient vessel to vent his frustrated
yearning for Honor on. And like that wasn't a slap
in the face?

But Tami felt like there was more to it. Yes, he'd
been watching Logan and Honor as they walked

by the windows last night, but she'd been getting a vibe off Keaton over the past several days that he was fighting with something internal. Was he attracted to her? Well, it had certainly felt that way last night. Was he prepared to do something about it? She pursed her lips slightly, remembering exactly what he'd done and how thoroughly. So while her first two questions had returned a positive response, that left her last question. Was he prepared to pursue this further? And to that she could only hear an empty, echoing *no* in the back of her mind.

She sighed and shifted her position. All of the above meant that to keep moving forward, she needed to remember to keep her physical distance and simply try to do her job to the best of her ability. There was no room to relive the embrace they'd shared. There was no way she could ever hope to explore that attraction, and that was for the best, wasn't it? Because, no matter how much she was attracted to Keaton Richmond, or how likely she would have been to fall into his arms and bed last night, if he'd offered them, she wasn't here to fall in love, or lust, or anything like that. She was here for one purpose only, and that was to feed information back to her father.

Her stomach pitched again as she made sure her seat was upright and her seat belt tight. At least she wasn't by the window on this trip. Keaton had offered to take the window seat when it had been clear they were going to have to sit together. He'd assiduously avoided brushing against her, right up until she'd fallen asleep all over him.

They'd no sooner landed when Keaton switched his phone from plane mode to regular service. The instant he'd done that, it began to ring. Tami tried to give him a little privacy while he answered, but it wasn't easy while they were still expected to be seated during taxi to the terminal.

"Hello? Yes, who?" He grimaced. "From which media outlet? Really?" He paused and listened for a few minutes. "That was the Everard pitch? Interesting." He paused again. "My comment on the Tanner project going to Everard Corporation? I have no comment."

He severed the call abruptly and looked across at his twin.

"What the hell was that all about?" Logan growled, looking fierce.

"It seems that Everard Corporation have preempted our offer for the Tanner project—and won—with a near identical pitch to our own."

Tami's stomach rolled.

"What do you mean they've gone with Everard Corporation? The tender wasn't due to close until tomorrow. And an identical pitch? What the hell?"

Logan sat up sharply and stared at his brother. His face was wreathed in lines of concern. Honor, too, looked worried.

"That bastard. Everard has to have a spy in our camp," Honor said in a shaking voice. "How else could he have done this?"

Keaton swore a blue streak. "This is going to play out very badly for us in the media. They're going to assume, like we do, that we have a mole, and that's going to damage all the work we've been doing to restore our company's name and reliability after Dad's double life was exposed. The fallout is going to hurt us far more than just financially."

Tami scrambled for the packet of ginger Honor had given her and popped another piece in her mouth to try and combat the rising bile that boiled up from inside her stomach. How had her father anticipated the Richmond bid so accurately? Keaton had only told her about it at dinner their first night in Sedona. She knew everything about the bid was being kept under wraps—in fact, it was being so closely guarded she hadn't heard anyone even discuss it during the team outdoor experience at all, and had only caught murmurs here and there between Fletcher Richmond and the three people sitting with her here.

And, more to the point, she hadn't told her father about anything she and Keaton had discussed during their intimate dinners together. Another sobering question flared in her mind. If her father had somehow acquired the information he needed without her help, where did that leave her with respect to the two and a half million he was supposed to be releasing from her trust fund?

Keaton ended the call, only to have his phone ring again immediately. He looked at his twin and grimaced.

"It's Mathias. Do you think he's heard the news? Fletcher will still be airborne for the next hour or so."

Tami had learned that Fletcher's younger brother, Mathias, together with their sister, Lisa, ran the east coast construction company Douglas Richmond had set up. It was almost an exact mirror in every way to the company that Logan, Keaton and Kristin operated in Seattle.

"Yeah, Kristin will have told him, I'm sure. Better deal with his call now. It's only going to get worse the longer you leave it," Logan said somberly.

"Yeah," Keaton agreed.

He answered the call. The words exchanged between the men were pithy and few.

"I promise you, I'll be conducting a full investigation starting the minute I'm back in the office. I suggest you do the same at your end."

Tami could hear the protest on the other end of the line.

"I don't believe any of my staff could be culpable, either, but someone had to have leaked the information to Everard. He's a sneaky bastard, but we will root out the traitor and there will be legal ramifications. Don't worry, we will make them pay. Corporate espionage will not be tolerated."

The plane had come to a full stop and the doors were being opened by the time he ended the call.

"We need to get straight to the office," he said to his brother and Honor. "When Fletcher hears the news, we need to be prepared. Mathias was mighty pissed off, but Fletcher is going to be apoplectic."

Tami was shaking. She couldn't be responsible for this somehow, could she? She had to talk to her father. She had to find out how he'd gotten the information he needed to preempt the Richmond offer with an identical one of his own.

It was late when she left the office. Keaton and his brother and sister were still locked in discussions in the boardroom, along with the head of IT, who had instigated a forensic investigation into the computer activity of all staff to see where any of the information may have been accessed and disseminated.

The anticipated blowup from Fletcher Richmond had been exactly what they'd expected. In the video call in the Richmond Developments boardroom, his fury had been incendiary and the relationship between the half siblings had become tenuous, with accusations about carelessness from one camp or the other being flung back and forth. Kristin had become the voice of reason, halting the flow of angry words between the four half brothers and their two half sisters, and reminding everyone they were all in this boat together. The only trouble was, with this development, the boat was rapidly sinking.

Tami had done her best to support them, but there'd been little she could do, aside from coordinate fresh water, hot beverages and food at regular intervals and take screeds of notes on her tablet. They were going to be at this for hours, and eventually Keaton had told her to head home. There was nothing more he needed her for.

While she knew the words weren't meant to be another blow to her already fragile state of mind, she couldn't help but feel them as such. She got into her car and sat there, exhaustion pulling at every part of her. As much as she wasn't looking forward to it, she still needed to meet with her father. She headed straight for her parents' home, relieved that even with the Friday night traffic, she could be there in half an hour.

Her parents' mansion, in the suburb of Magnolia, was lit up like a Christmas tree. There was no conserving power or anything like that in Warren Everard's world. No, he wanted everyone to see, carbon footprint or no, just how powerful and successful he was at all times. Tami spoke in the speaker box at the entrance and waited as the heavy wrought-iron gates, embellished with her father's initials in gold leaf, swung open. She drove through, and in the rearview mirror, watched as the gates swung closed again.

The burning sensation in her stomach, which had started on landing at SeaTac midday, ratcheted up a few notches, and after she pulled up by the ornate portico at the front door, she reached in her bag for the crystalized ginger. The packet was empty. It had been that kind of day. She was going to have to do this without the benefit of anything to help settle her stomach.

Tami forced herself from the car and went to the front door. Her father's butler, an anachronism in this modern age, waited in the open doorway for her.

"Good evening, Sanders. I need to talk with my father rather urgently."

"He's expecting you. You'll find him in the den."

Tami's stomach burned that little bit more fiercely. Her father was waiting for her? How did he even know she was back? Had his spies at Richmond Developments told him? This was worse than she'd anticipated. She crossed the black-and-white marble-floored entrance, her footsteps echoing in the two-story foyer, as she made her way to her father's den.

She hesitated a moment at the door, remembering the many times she'd been summoned to this room to be castigated over her latest failure. But, she reminded herself, she wasn't that cowed child anymore. She was an adult who'd been independent of her parents since she was eighteen—well, independent until she'd needed two and a half million dollars, she reminded herself. And that gave her two and a half million reasons to face up to her father and demand to know what he'd done. She knocked sharply and pushed the door open before her father could respond.

He was seated in a wingback chair in front of a burning fire. Not for the first time, Tami saw every aspect of him and his life as one cliché after another. Aside from her coloring, she'd inherited very little of the man sitting there with a smug expression… and she was painfully glad of it. She never wanted to be anything like him.

"I see you got what you wanted with the Tanner development," she said bluntly.

"I did. I imagine they're a little upset at Richmond Developments and DR Construction right now."

He laughed. It was a nasty sound that grated on Tami's ears. How could he take so much joy in this? His actions had been underhanded and would cost jobs and livelihoods for so many people who were already in shaky circumstances.

"How did you circumvent the tender process?" she demanded.

He waved a meaty hand in the air. "A minor detail. The thing is, I won."

"Yes, you did. That means you can release my trust fund to me now."

"Oh, how so?"

"It was what we agreed. When you got the information you wanted—which you obviously did somehow, because from what I understand your pitch was identical in virtually every way to what the Richmond pitch was going to be—I'd get access to my fund."

"Ah, but you're forgetting something."

"What?"

"*You* didn't specifically give me the information I asked for. In fact, if I remember correctly, you ignored most of my messages and calls requesting updates, and only replied in a series of painfully short and noninformative texts, did you not?"

She swallowed and nodded. It was no use telling him now that she'd planned to write up all the notes she'd made on her phone.

"Then you didn't deliver on your side of the deal,

did you?" He shook his head with a sardonic smile pulling at his lips. "Tami, Tami, Tami. You'll never learn, will you? To survive in this world you have got to be more cutthroat. You won't win anything by being a doormat."

"I'm not a doormat," she argued.

No matter how hard she tried to ignore her father's baiting techniques, and he had many of them, she always rose to them, giving him the satisfaction of winning every darn time.

"You're both a doormat and a disappointment. And you can forget access to your fund. Your grandmother did the right thing appointing me as your trustee. Obviously, you lack the clarity of foresight and wisdom required to manage such a sum of money." He made a derogatory sound. "Giving it all to a charity, what the hell were you thinking? No, wait, don't bother telling me because we both know you never think things through and it's because of your failings that you got yourself in this situation."

"I was used," she protested.

Used by someone as scurrilous as your father, a little voice jeered in the back of her mind.

"Yes, used because you're too darn trusting for your own good. You can leave now. And don't bother showing your face here again until you develop some backbone."

"Just because I don't choose to stomp all over people doesn't mean I don't have a backbone."

"Sure, you keep telling yourself that. And while you're at it, ask yourself why, when you encountered a problem, the first person you came running to was me."

He got up from his chair and walked past her and out of the den, leaving her standing there, seething in silence. She refused to let the cruelty of his words sink any deeper. She had enough worries on her plate now. Our People, Our Homes had a fiduciary duty to report the theft of the money from their coffers to their donors and to the necessary authorities. Even though she'd been the innocent dupe, she *had* made her computer password available to Mark, and by doing so had given him access to the file where she'd kept the charity's banking password and access code, as well. Both those actions had been in breach of her user agreement, which had been designed precisely to protect that kind of data.

Tami turned and made her way out of the house, barely even acknowledging Sanders's polite "good evening" as he let her out the front door. What on earth was she going to do? For now, she still had a job to do at Richmond Developments, but in all honesty she couldn't keep her initial intentions secret from Keaton anymore. If he knew the lengths to which her father was prepared to go to win whatever it was that he'd set his sights on, even going so far as to use his daughter, then maybe he could find out exactly how her dad had finagled their tender details so precisely. She had to tell him about the person her father had positioned in HR for a start. And who knew how many other spies he'd positioned within the company?

And then there was Our People, Our Homes. She had to tell them she couldn't make good on her promise. Suddenly, the meeting she'd just had with her father seemed like child's play compared to what she had yet to face.

Keaton was at his office long before the sun began to rise as he had been every day for the past week. He cradled his mug of coffee in both hands and stared out the window at the awakening city. He loved this place—the city, the state, the country. But most of all he loved Richmond Developments and he hated to see it crumbling on his watch. It didn't matter that the responsibility was shared between himself and his siblings. It didn't matter that it was circumstances beyond their control that had started the downward slide—it mattered that it was happening while he was at the helm and he was going to do whatever it took to make things right again.

And it mattered that they were still no closer to discovering exactly who had been behind the leaked information that had rocked them to their very foundation. As anticipated, the media had been having a field day with speculation about what had gone so wrong here at Richmond Developments.

He heard a sound in the outer office. It would be Tami. He wasn't surprised she'd come in early. She'd been in early every day this last week, even over the weekend. At least that shell-shocked look she'd worn the day they came home from Sedona had finally left her, and each day she had done her best to offer as much support as she could. He thought about the way he'd spoken with her lately. He'd been abrupt on most occasions, which had been unfair. It wasn't her fault that things had gone pear-shaped. He turned away from the window, set his mug on his desk and went through to the outer office.

She was settled at her desk, looking immaculately groomed in the dark navy suit she'd worn on her first day here. Corporate Tami was quite a change from the jeans and casual tops he'd grown accustomed to seeing her in while they were in Sedona, but no less attractive from his point of view, either. He snapped his mind back to attention. He was not going down that route. They'd drawn their line in the sand. Regrettably, his body hadn't gotten the memo.

Even from the back, she stirred him. She'd swept her hair up into a tight roll at the back of her head, which exposed the slender, elegant line of her neck—a neck made for nuzzling, his libido teased him. A neck made to be ignored, his more pragmatic brain responded promptly. It would be best to face her, he decided, so he walked quickly around her desk. She looked up immediately.

Keaton felt as if he'd been punched in the gut. She looked terrible. Her skin was pale and there were violet shadows beneath her hazel eyes that spoke of yet another rough night. She was taking this hard. Guilt tore at his chest. Or had he done this to her?

"What can I do for you, Keaton?" she asked.

Even her voice sounded weary, and although she smiled there was nothing of the vibrant, cheerful character she'd demonstrated as they'd tackled challenge after challenge during their outdoor pursuits.

"Are you well, Tami?"

"You mean, I look like something the dog dragged in, right?"

There was a sardonic twist to her mouth that was out of keeping with the woman he'd come to know. The woman he'd kissed. The woman he'd wanted with every cell in his body, but denied himself.

"I won't lie—you've looked better."

This time her lips curved into a more genuine smile and a snort of laughter escaped her.

"Well, thank you, I think. I had a bad night is all," she said, glossing over her shattered appearance. "Now, I imagine we have plenty of work to do today. Where do you want me to start?"

He was both relieved and disappointed that she was all business. The practical side of him started dictating a list of orders. Contracts that they needed to follow up on, tenders they were awaiting responses on, suppliers they needed to woo to ensure they received the best prices. By the time she got through the list he would hopefully have a stronger handle on where Richmond Developments would be heading in the next few weeks.

"Oh, and Logan and Kristin will be in shortly. Can you get someone to rustle up some coffee and breakfast bagels for us?"

"Of course. Is that all for now?"

He blinked. Wow, she was all business all right. "Yes, thank you. That will be all for now."

Feeling as if he'd missed a golden opportunity, but unsure exactly as to what that opportunity was, he returned to his office and closed the door. She was different. Untouchable. No, that wasn't the right word, she was eminently touchable, but there was a fragility about her right now that made him feel as though if he did touch her, she might shatter into a million tiny shards.

Surely, she wasn't this invested in Richmond Developments already that losing the Tanner project had impacted her to this degree? Or maybe she really was. She'd certainly been interested about expressing her ideas when they'd discussed it during their first dinner in Sedona.

But all that bright enthusiasm had very thoroughly been quelled. Was that his fault? Had he been too harsh when he'd stepped away after that kiss? Of course he had. He'd been angry at himself for not resisting the temptation she offered—angry, even, at her for simply being there and tempting him in the first place. All of it had been unfair and unreasonable. They'd kissed. No one died. He could have handled it way better. He should be pleased about her obvious professionalism, given the fact that he'd been the one to reach for her and kiss her like a man starved of a lifetime of affection.

He picked up his coffee mug again and took a sip, then twisted his mouth in disgust at the now cold brew.

He'd been the one to pull back. He'd been the one to say he'd overstepped and that it wouldn't happen again. She'd agreed. That was that. Done, dusted, over before anything could begin.

So why did he feel like he'd lost something special now? He had exactly what he wanted. Didn't he?

Eight

Things were beginning to show promise, aside from the fact that they'd lost several more key staff members in the aftermath of losing the Tanner project. There was always more work to pitch for, even in a depressed market, and while things weren't as buoyant as they would have been if they'd taken on the Tanner job, they weren't exactly heading to the financial wall, either.

The main fly in Keaton's ointment these days was the complete lack of so much as a thread of information to lead him to whoever had fed their tender details to Everard Corporation. And that lack of information made Keaton edgy. Who could be trusted? It didn't create the best working atmosphere, no matter how many teams they'd sent to Sedona. That said, at least they'd managed to patch up the wrenching hole that had opened up between them and their half siblings. And that had put them in an even stronger position when it came to pitching for projects nationwide. Their joint reputations counted for a lot and Keaton was eternally grateful that, for all that their father's deception had destroyed, his children had had the grace and strength to pull everything together cohesively.

He and Tami were working late, again. Each day he'd given her the opportunity to leave on time, but she'd been dogged in her determination to match him hour for hour at the office. The shadows under her eyes remained, but were slightly less noticeable these past couple of days, but something still clearly troubled her. In those moments when she wasn't one-hundred-percent focused on her work, it was as if her mind would drift somewhere else and she'd get a deeply worried expression on her face. If he asked her if anything was amiss, she'd merely cover it up, smile and say everything was okay.

But everything was very definitely not okay. With every day they worked together, he only wanted her more and that knowledge was like a thorn in his side. Other people made office romances work, but Keaton didn't want to lay himself bare like that again. Trouble was, no one but Tami interested him in that way. Not a single other woman drew him to her, as she did. And when he thought about it, he hadn't even felt this way about Honor. Their relationship had been convenient on every level, but not passionate. Not spontaneous. It had been structured and balanced and about as boring as a spreadsheet, now that he came to think about it.

Oh, sure, they'd have made things work, if they'd stayed together, but seeing her glow under Logan's care and attention showed Keaton exactly how little they'd offered each other. He was glad for Honor now, even though it had meant her cheating on him for them to discover they weren't right for each other. Occasionally, watching Honor and Logan together, it still stung just a little, but that was more a matter of pride than anything else.

With Tami, however, he'd struck a wall he had no idea of how to get through. A wall of his own making, he reminded himself as he looked up to see her enter his office. Keaton cast a look at the ornate hanging clock and was shocked to see it was already 9:00 p.m.

"Here's that data analysis you and Fletcher asked for. Would you like to go over it first, before I send it through to him?"

"No, send it to me and I'll go through it with him tomorrow. It's late, we both need to call it quits for the day."

"Are you sure? I still have those figures to run on the—"

"Tami," he interrupted. "Stop. Sit." He waited until she sat down in the chair opposite his desk. "Now, take a breath."

"I take breaths all the time."

"But you, and I, have been working double time

in this past week. I think we both need to think about cutting back to normal hours."

"Seriously, Keaton, that report will only take me a minute to—"

"Tomorrow," he interrupted again. "Now, how about we go and grab something to eat together somewhere. I know you haven't had dinner yet and I'm starved. How about it?"

For a moment he thought she'd refuse, but then she nodded.

"You want to go now?"

"It's as good a time as any," he said with a shrug.

"I'll just go freshen up and I'll be back in a couple of minutes."

She was true to her word, and on her return he escorted her down in the elevator and out the front of the building.

"Good night, Stan," he called to the late-shift security guard at the main counter.

"Good night, sir, Ms. Wilson."

Tami smiled and gave the man a slight wave before turning to Keaton. "Are we going somewhere in walking distance?"

"No," he answered and gestured to the car waiting outside. "I made a booking and called a ride. We deserve to go somewhere special after how hard we've both been working."

"Okay," she answered warily. "But I'm not dressed for anywhere too high-end."

"It's not, don't worry. It'll be good food in a great setting."

When they pulled up outside the lakeside restaurant, he saw Tami's lips curl up in a smile of approval.

"Oh, I love this place!"

"Yeah, it's one of my favorites, too. I love Asian fusion. The best of everything."

They went into the restaurant and were quickly shown to their table. It was cramped quarters, but the glittering view out over the lake was second to none, and if the aromas from the kitchen were anything to go by, they were in for a treat. They didn't waste a lot of time on the menu—both of them were hungry and ready to order the moment their server returned. Both of them eschewed wine, opting instead for mineral water.

"You've been working really hard, Tami," he said as he leaned back in his chair as they waited for their dishes to arrive. "I really appreciate how quickly you've settled into your role."

"I try my hardest to fit in."

There was a hint of sorrow in her eyes and he hastened to assure her that she was doing great.

"Seriously, it was a lucky day for us when you started as my assistant."

She didn't hold his gaze, but fiddled with her napkin as if it was the most important thing on the planet right now.

"I can't help noticing that you're not yourself, though. Is everything okay?" he pressed.

As he expected, her lips lifted in an approximation of a smile. But he could tell that while she assured him everything was fine, something was still bugging her. Was it the kiss they'd shared that last night in Sedona? Or something else?

"Tami, you'd tell me if there was something bothering you, right? I mean, I know I can come across as a bit single-minded about things, but you can always approach me if you need to."

"I know. And everything's fine, just fine."

If she said it often enough, maybe it would be true, right? The investigation had begun into the missing funds from Our People, Our Homes, and she'd been given an appointment time to go into the police station and answer questions. It wouldn't be long before the news got out that she was involved, and once that happened, she'd no doubt be fired from Richmond Developments. It was strange, she thought. She'd been so nervous about her role working for Keaton, and thought she'd miss her work with the charity much more, but she found the cut and thrust of Keaton's work fascinating from a peripheral perspective. And her support role was something she enjoyed and knew she excelled at.

Watching Keaton work was something in itself. He attacked things with purpose and with a clear result always in sight, and he wasn't afraid to change direction if something wasn't working. The support of Logan and Kristin in their roles as joint CEOs made the three of them even stronger and their style was so different to anything she'd witnessed before. Success-driven, but always with an eye to the social benefits their work would produce. She could see Richmond Developments and DR Construction rising from their current funk and reassuming their position among the strongest players in the construction and development markets. It felt great to be a part of that and she wanted to remain there. And the fact it was a metaphoric middle finger to her father gave her no small amount of satisfaction.

There was also the fact that working there paid very well and with limited savings and no other income to speak of, she needed the funds. She knew it wouldn't last forever. Not when the truth came out, and as much as she wasn't looking forward to it, she knew she had to come clean. Even if she hadn't been the person who'd actually given her father the information, she had intended to. Living each day on tenterhooks was taking its toll on her, but she also knew that if she'd just up and left immediately when they'd returned from Sedona it would have made her look even guiltier. No, she would tell him the truth, in her own time.

Her attention returned to the man sitting opposite her. She admired Keaton on so many levels and felt herself drawn to him more every day. It was all she could do to keep her head down and focused on her work each day, when all she wanted to do was relive that kiss they'd shared, right before he'd rejected her. No, that wasn't fair. Even then, he'd done the noble thing and taken all the blame for their kiss. A kiss that lived in her subconscious and plagued her fractured sleep with the memory of his touch, his taste, his warmth. At least by doing her job to the best of her ability, she was making herself indispensable, proving she was capable of being an adult about their embrace and that she could carry on as if it hadn't totally rocked her world. And that way, his suggestion that she either leave or take on another role within the company, away from him, would not come to pass.

And when he found out that her father had been responsible for her appointment? She swallowed against the fear that threatened to close her throat. She hoped that when she eventually told him that he'd listen to the truth that she never wanted to be a spy and that she wasn't the cause of the loss of the Tanner project. But when her involvement with Our People, Our Homes became public knowledge…? She swallowed again. Living with the fear of him discovering her secrets was just about giving her a stomach ulcer. She could only hope that her diligence would speak volumes as to her dedication to both her job and to him.

Thankfully, their dishes began to arrive at the table and she was saved from further discussion as they started on their meal. Conversation fell away as they began to sample the dishes. Keaton ate the same way he kissed, with great attention to detail and savoring the minutest aspects. A swell of desire flowed through her, making her shift a little in her seat. She had to stop thinking about him like that, she growled at herself as she bit into a succulent shrimp and let the flavors dance along her taste buds. He'd made it clear there could be nothing between them, and given what had happened with Honor Gould, she wasn't surprised.

She, too, should be more wary of office romances, especially after the way Mark Pennington had used her before disappearing and smearing her name in the process. And yet, she could barely take her eyes off Keaton as they shared the platters of food. Wariness be damned, she thought. Every now and then, life threw chances your way and if you were too scared to reach out and grab them, you deserved to get nothing in the end. With that in mind, she decided to force Keaton to talk—really talk—about their time in Sedona, especially that kiss. She felt as if it was an elephant in the room every day at work and she wanted to deal with it head-on and get it out of the way for good.

"This is good, huh?" she asked, opening the conversation again.

"So good. I didn't realize how hungry I was. I imagine you're just the same."

"Are you referring to my obscenely huge appetite back in Sedona," she said with a smile.

There, she'd done it. She'd injected Sedona into the conversation. Now, to keep it on track.

"Hey, nothing obscene about a healthy appetite," he said, helping himself to more of the shrimp dish.

"I really enjoyed the trip there and meeting some of the DR Construction team. Making those connections has really helped with sharing information these past couple of weeks. What would you say your favorite part of the whole experience was?"

She stared at him expectantly.

"I'd say the kayaking on the river. I know those rapids were child's play in the grand scheme of things, but it was fun. I bet your favorite part was the zip lining, am I right?" He grinned at her and waited for her reply.

"No, actually. While that really ranked up there, there's another moment that meant a lot to me."

"Oh, what was that?"

His fork halted halfway to his mouth and he watched her, waiting for her to explain.

"It was when you kissed me."

She felt the air between them thicken and Keaton slowly lowered his fork to his plate.

"Tami, I—"

She raised a finger to silence him. "Please, hear me out. I know you felt as if you went too far—I can understand that. I also know why you probably don't want to enter into a new office romance."

"Ah, so the office grapevine has been working as efficiently as ever, I see," he said with no small amount of irritation.

"That aside, I feel like the whole situation has put some kind of invisible wall between us. And it's one that needs to come down if we're to be able to continue to work efficiently together. I don't want you to feel as if you have to walk on eggshells around me. I won't deny that your kiss totally blew me away. It did. And if I had the chance to repeat it, I'd grab it with both hands." She smiled. "Kind of like the way I'd like to grab you. I can and do accept that you feel it's inappropriate for us to have a relationship, but can we at least have some semblance of friendship? You know, figure out a way to accept we're attracted to one another and work around it, anyway?"

Keaton leaned back in his chair and took his time responding. She was beginning to worry she'd gone too far with her honesty, but then he leaned forward again and, to her surprise, he took her hand from where it rested on the table and held it in his.

"I don't want to be friends with you, Tami. I want more than that, way more, but by your own admission you can see why that wouldn't work for us."

She curled her fingers around his and squeezed gently. "I know, but we can do much better than we've been doing, can't we?"

"Of course we can," he agreed and let go of her hand.

It was a start, she conceded. Maybe not quite the start she'd hoped for, but he'd admitted he wanted more than friendship. It was his own stubborn personal rules that were holding him back. Okay, she could respect that. It wouldn't be easy, but at least they had it out in the open.

When their meal was done, Keaton booked a ride share to take them home. As they waited in the cold outside the restaurant, a chilling wind blew off the lake and Tami shivered a little. She was startled when Keaton put his arm around her and drew her closer to his body.

"We don't both need to freeze," he said by way of explanation. "Why don't you snuggle into me a bit more. We've still got a few minutes before the car will be here."

"Or we could wait inside the restaurant lobby?" she suggested perversely.

She turned into him so they were chest-to-chest, and could already feel the heat of his body permeating her suit and seeping in to her skin to warm her up. He looked back and the movement caused cold air to filter in between them.

"Not with that massive line of people waiting for tables," he said. "Looks like you'll have to make do with me instead, or freeze. Friends, remember? We have to look out for each other."

"I…" She hesitated a moment, afraid that all her longing would coalesce into whatever she said next. "I'll make do with you."

He laughed, and the movement of his chest made her nipples rub against the cups of her bra and stand to attention. Mortification filled her. What if he noticed? Her blouse and suit were designed for a climate-controlled office, not a cold March Seattle night. At least she could always put it down to the cold, right? Even though her body's reaction had nothing to do with the temperature and everything to do with him.

He checked his phone again. "Hmm, our ride must be stuck in traffic. Looks like we'll be waiting a while longer. You okay with that?"

His breath was warm against the top of her head and she nodded, barely trusting herself to speak.

"Why don't you wrap your arms around my waist?" he suggested.

"Are you sure?" she asked, surprised.

"Hey, it's cold. I'm doing the right thing by my employee in keeping her warm, aren't I?"

"Whatever you say, boss," she said as lightly as she could, but her voice broke on the last word.

Even though every particle of her body urged her to take him at his word, she took her time hugging more deeply into his body. He was right, though. Their shared warmth made a difference. Keaton slipped his phone back into his jacket pocket and closed his arms around her, too. To anyone watching, they'd look like any other loving couple on the side of the road, but Tami was all too aware that they were not a couple, no matter how much they'd cleared the air at dinner.

After another few minutes, she realized that she was not the only one being physically affected by their nearness. There was a distinct pressure against her lower belly. She must have moved slightly because she felt a puff of air escape Keaton's lips.

"Sorry," he said in a strangled voice. "Can't help nature."

"Would you like me to move?" she asked, leaning back a little and angling her head up to look at his face.

Trouble was, her movement saw her pelvis press in a little more firmly against his lower regions and the contact sent a spiral of longing deep to her core.

"Tami, I…" He sucked in a harsh breath. "It seems that no matter how hard I try, I just can't resist you."

He looked down at her and she watched as a tumult of emotions crossed his face. First, helplessness, then a little frustration, and finally, acceptance, which was quickly followed by what she privately called his decision expression. When he bent his head toward her she knew what was coming. Knew it, ached for it, welcomed it.

His lips closed on hers, the pressure at first soft and gentle, then she opened her lips in response and kissed him back with all the longing she'd bottled up since they'd left Sedona and with deeper demand. Her fingers tightened on the fine cotton of his shirt and beneath them she felt the muscles of his back. His strong hands pressed her more firmly against him and she relished the heat of his body against her torso. His tongue stroked hers and right now, everything about her focused on that point of their bodies. It all began and ended with Keaton in that moment. It was only when a car horn sounded beside them that she remembered where they were.

Keaton was breathing heavily as he wrenched his lips from hers.

"It's our ride."

She started to pull away, but he stopped her.

"Before we get in the car, I just want to say something. I won't apologize for that kiss and I won't pretend it didn't happen. These past two weeks have been torture and I haven't been able to stop thinking about the last time we kissed. I've tried to fight it, but it's a losing battle. In fact, it's a battle I want to cede. The hell with being friends. I want you, Tami. I want to make love to you, I want to lose myself in you, and see you lose yourself in me, so we can forget for a while. I won't hold it against you if you say no. I will respect whatever decision you make, but when we get in that car, do I give the driver both of our addresses, or just mine?"

She hesitated a few seconds, her insides jumping with a weird combination of heated desire and a healthy dose of caution. If they did this, it would change everything about their working relationship. Everything about *them*. It was a line she had told herself she would never cross again, and she believed Keaton had felt the same way. And now they felt the same about each other. She took a deep breath.

"Yours."

"Thank you," he said, and kissed her fiercely on the top of her head.

Keaton took her hand and led her to the car, opening the door for her and following her into the back seat. Their driver wished them a good evening, then focused on his route while Tami and Keaton sat, fingers entwined and bodies humming with anticipation, as they traveled the dark streets to his apartment building on the other side of the lake. The journey didn't take long, which was just as well, Tami told herself. She wasn't certain if it was because she was grasping this opportunity with both hands to show Keaton how much she felt for him, or because if the journey had taken any longer she might have changed her mind.

But she'd spent too much time regretting her choices and her actions in life, and she was determined to take this night to express how her feelings for him had developed. Even if she never said the words, she would show Keaton with every breath, every touch, every thought she was capable of, how much she admired him and how much he meant to her. She knew he was an honorable man—the way he conducted himself at work was a prime example. That she was less honorable was something she'd have to sweep under a metaphorical rug for now and hope against hope that their lovemaking tonight would show him the real Tami. The one who wanted to belong. The one who wanted to love freely. The one who would be loyal without question if only given the chance.

Tension vibrated off Keaton in waves as they traveled up in the elevator to his penthouse suite. The minute they were through the door, he pressed her against the wall and hungrily kissed her again. Tami tangled her fingers in his hair, holding him to her, not wanting to let him go. She felt his hands at the lapels of her jacket and let go of him only long enough for him to peel the garment from her shoulders and down her arms, and then she was touching him again. His fingers were nimble on the buttons of her blouse and it fell open, revealing the simple balconette bra she wore beneath it.

Maybe she should have splashed out on something

more elaborate, indulged herself, but judging by the expression on his face as he looked at her creamy skin swelling above the pale pink cups rimmed with the merest froth of lace, she knew it wouldn't have made any difference.

"I want to touch you," he said in a voice that had grown deep with longing. "Everywhere."

"I want you to touch me, too," she answered.

He bent to press his lips against the swell of one breast and inhaled.

"You smell so damn good," he murmured against her skin.

"Why am I still wearing too many clothes?" she said with a small laugh.

He snorted in response and she felt his hands move around her ribs to the fastening of her bra. In seconds, he had it loose and he tugged her blouse and bra free of her breasts, exposing them to his hungry gaze. Tami felt her nipples tighten in response and an ache filled her, an ache that she knew would only be assuaged by his touch, his possession. And she ached to touch him, too.

"We're both wearing too many clothes," Keaton murmured with a smile as he straightened to his full height. "Come with me. We're not doing this in my entranceway."

This turned out to be a slow disrobing of one another in the dimness of his bedroom, while outside the city lights glittered below them. Tami felt goose bumps rise on her skin as he divested her of her last item of clothing and she stood naked in front of him. Her eyes roamed his naked form. She'd already known he was beautifully chiseled from watching him while they rock-climbed, with strong arms and a flat stomach and powerful legs, but seeing him completely naked was enough to rob her of coherent thought.

His erection jutted proudly from a nest of dark blond hair and she stepped forward, feeling the heat of him against her bare body before they even touched.

"You're beautiful," she whispered, lifting one hand to trace the muscles of his upper arms, then his chest, then lower.

"Beautiful…no. That word is reserved for you," he said gruffly.

He lifted his hand to her hair and slowly pulled out each pin that held it in the tight roll that she wore for work every day. He filtered his fingers through her locks, shaking them loose from the confines of the brutally tight twist, and massaged her scalp.

"There, that's better," he said.

Then his hands dropped to her shoulders and he carefully edged her back toward the bed. They stopped when the back of her legs made contact and he coaxed her down onto the broad surface, letting his fingers drift softly over her, back and forth and back and forth, until she was squirming with need.

"Come to me," she said. "I want to touch you, too."

"Next time," he answered. "For now I want to

revel in you. Let me make you mindless. Let me chase away the shadows I see in your eyes every day."

His words were a balm to her soul and she allowed him his wish. His hands were gentle and soft at first, then sure and firm as he explored her shoulders, her arms, her breasts and then, finally, her hips and upper thighs. She was wet with longing and let her legs drop open as his touch skimmed her mound. The palm of his hand brushed against her clitoris and it was as if he'd set off an electrical surge through her body. She felt her hips lift off the bed as she sought the release she so desperately wanted.

"You like that, huh?" he murmured softly. "Let's see if you like this more."

He skimmed her again before shifting his touch to between her legs. His fingers probed her, and then, slick with her wetness, he slid one finger inside her body. Her inner muscles clenched on the welcome invasion, but still it wasn't enough.

"More...of you. I need more," she begged.

"Your wish is my command."

She felt the mattress dip a little as he shifted over her and heard the tear of a foil packet as he took care of protection. Tami reached for him as he positioned himself between her legs.

"I had planned to take a little longer over this," he said with a rueful smile.

"Next time," she said. "Now, please—now."

He maintained eye contact as he guided his erection to her entrance. She moaned as he teased her by nudging her with his swollen tip.

"More," she demanded, her voice guttural with need.

And then he gave her more, and more, and more. Over and over until she lost all sense of being and plummeted over the edge of here and now and into a realm of pleasure the likes of which she'd rarely known before. She hooked her legs around his hips, not wanting him to stop even as the pulsing waves of her climax pounded through her. When Keaton came, his entire body went rigid, his muscles straining as he groaned in relief, his hips surging against her as if he could never get deep enough, be part of her enough, before easing to a halt.

He collapsed against her and she relished the weight of his body on hers, the scent of his skin, the throb of his heart as it beat in unison with hers. Tami clung to his shoulders as though he was the only thing keeping her anchored at this point in time. And maybe he was. Her world had been in turmoil for weeks and this moment with him had been the most real and grounding experience of her life. He might have suggested it as respite, but Tami knew that, for her, at least, it was so much more than that.

Keaton rolled to one side, taking her with him. His gray eyes were solemn as he stared at her.

"This changes everything, Tami, you know that."

"Shh," she said, placing her forefinger on his lips. "Let's not analyze this. Let's just take tonight…for us. Everything else can wait."

He was silent a moment, then nodded. "Okay. Let's take tonight. I'll be right back."

He rolled off the bed and walked through to what

she assumed was an en suite bathroom. When he returned she let her eyes roam over the contours of his body. He truly was magnificent. And, for tonight, he was hers and she didn't plan to waste a minute of it.

Nine

Tami watched as the digital clock changed from 4:59 to 5:00. She'd been watching each minute roll over for the past hour and no matter how much she thought and worried and obsessed, nothing had changed.

Trust meant everything to Keaton, and she'd taken all he could give her and she was about to throw it all back in his face. It had been selfish to accept his lovemaking, she knew that. And the truth she had to share with him would shred any chance they had of having a relationship or any kind of future together. She had to do it—she had to tell him. She couldn't go forward with the ugly truth of her reason for working for him being kept hidden away.

But how to start? What to say?

Keaton was lying on the mattress, deep in sleep. The sheets were tangled around his waist and Tami took every care not to disturb him as she slid from the bed and tiptoed around to pick up her clothing, including going out to the entrance of the apartment to retrieve her bra, blouse and jacket. She let herself into the half bath off the entrance and gave herself a quick wash, then dragged on her clothes.

Her hair was a mess, her throat pink in patches where Keaton's beard had left its mark. She touched her throat with trembling fingers. She'd relished every moment of last night, but she was terrified now that the memories would be as fleeting as these reminders of Keaton's passion. She swallowed and blinked back the burn of tears in her eyes.

No one had forced her to do this. She could have just let Our People, Our Homes commence their investigation right from the start. But she'd taken personal responsibility for what had happened and seen it equally as her responsibility to make restitution. But her ability to do that had been hindered by her father the way he'd tried to block and stifle every single thing she'd ever tried to do. She should have known he'd do whatever he could to see her fail again.

She stared at her face in the mirror. She was every bit as weak as her father had always said she was. She was the one who'd approached him for an easy out instead of facing the consequences of her choices. And she was the one who'd agreed to his conditions without any consideration as to the effect of her actions. She'd put Keaton and his family's businesses at risk. And even though she'd wanted to make everything right and she'd ended up making everything wrong instead.

She knew now, she loved him. Deeply, completely. And, feeling as she did, she couldn't continue to live the lie she'd agreed to perpetuate for her father. It was past time to take ownership of what she'd done. This thing with Keaton couldn't go any further with her deception lying like a coiled snake between them. Even though it meant she'd be getting into a whole world of trouble—trouble that would likely double as the investigation into the missing funds at Our People, Our Homes deepened. She had no doubt that Richmond Developments would take legal action against her. She couldn't hide from any of it. Not even the anger she knew she'd see on Keaton's face when she told him the whole truth. She deserved it, and as much as it would flay her heart, she had to take this step.

Tami squared her shoulders and turned out the light before making her way to the living room. There she sat, staring out the window until the gray light of dawn began to streak the Seattle skyline. A movement in the hallway alerted her to Keaton's presence and the fierce burning sensation in her stomach ratcheted up another notch.

"You're up early," he commented with a yawn. "Couldn't sleep?"

She watched as he rubbed his jaw with one hand, heard the rasp of whiskers on skin. She would take each of these memories and tuck them away, because she knew once she told him what she had to, that they would be all she had left.

"Keaton," she said on a sigh. "We need to talk."

All signs of slumber disappeared from his face and his eyes sharpened instantly.

"Talk? Why do I get the feeling I'm not going to like what you have to say?"

"Because you won't. I should have been upfront with you before we got to this."

Despite the fact that he wore nothing but a pair of pajama bottoms and his hair was still tousled from her fingers running through it, his demeanor changed instantly to that of the corporate warrior he truly was at heart. Somehow, that made it easier. Seeing the expression on his face and the closed body language was all so much easier to face than the sexy man, warm from sleep and still bearing the marks of her fingernails on his shoulders from when he'd driven her mad with desire and pleasure and all the things she didn't deserve.

"Well, spit it out," he said sharply.

"I think I need to go to the beginning. To when I started at Richmond Developments. You see, my appointment there wasn't everything it seemed."

He raised one sardonic brow and crossed his arms across his bare torso. "Carry on."

"My father is Warren Everard."

She could see a muscle working in Keaton's jaw, but he remained silent. His eyes, however, flashed with barely repressed fury. The burn in her stomach increased.

"You don't go by your father's name," he said bluntly.

"No, I don't. I changed my name twelve years ago when I decided I no longer wanted to be associated with him."

She took in a shallow breath, then another. She could guess what Keaton would say next and he, true to form, didn't disappoint.

"And yet you became his puppet?" His voice seethed with repressed fury.

"I, um, asked him a favor. In repayment, I agreed to be positioned in your employment and to feed him information."

"That was you? You're responsible for us losing the Tanner project?"

Keaton's voice had reverted to being flat and clipped, but she had no doubt as to the emotions behind his words.

Loathing.

Disgust.

Anger.

"I have no idea how he got the information, but it wasn't from me," she said in a level voice that didn't betray the near overwhelming flutter of nerves in her chest.

"You seriously expect me to believe that?"

Tami rose on shaking legs and stood her ground. "Believe what you want—I know what's true."

He sneered. "True? Really? You have the gall to say that when you were your father's spy?"

She swallowed back the bile that threatened to flood her mouth. "I know you're mad at me—"

"Mad? You think I'm mad? Oh, I'm way past mad. You're going to regret this. I will use all the legal might I have at my disposal to make you pay for your treachery. Your actions cost us millions—worse, you've cost *decent* people their livelihoods."

"Keaton, please. Hear me out. My father has at least one other person positioned in the office that I know of. Someone in HR. That's how I got the role. I'm not certain who it is, but I suspect it was the woman I met on my first day—Monique. If she's working for my father, she could have filtered a lot more people into Richmond Developments who are reporting back to him, too."

"You can be sure there will be a thorough audit of staff, but out of everyone, you were the one outside of our family that I talked to about the Tanner project. Not anyone else. Just you."

"Keaton, I'm sorry. I never expected—"

"Never expected what, exactly? To lie? To deceive? To deliberately earn my trust with that sweet little speech at dinner last night and then shove it back down my throat? To see my company potentially crumble into dust while allowing your father's firm to scoop up business that we'd all but won? Interesting, when that's exactly what you set out to do.

"Congratulations, you are truly your father's daughter. I hope he's proud of you. You've not only betrayed me, but you've betrayed every honest person working for my family. I don't know how you can live with yourself. You no longer hold a position at Richmond Developments and you are in gross breach of your employment contract. Expect to hear from our company lawyers on Monday. Now, get out of my home."

She knew there was nothing left to say or do so she grabbed her handbag and started to leave. Keaton's voice stopped her as she reached the door.

"Why now?"

"What?"

"Why tell me now?" Keaton demanded.

There was a note of anguish in his voice that made her insides coil in a knot. She'd done this to him. She'd betrayed him, hurt him and ruined everything.

Tami drew in a deep breath and let the truth fall from her lips. "Because I realized that I've fallen in love with you and I couldn't keep working for you with that between us. I only wanted to do what was right, Keaton."

There was more, so much more she ached to tell him, but she knew if he now heard about what had happened at Our People, Our Homes, he'd never believe she had been an unwitting pawn in that disaster. As it was, the expression on his face grew even darker.

"Haven't you told enough lies already? I don't need to hear your clichés," he said, his lips twisting in a bitter line. "Leave. I don't want to see you again."

The security guard was waiting for her when the elevator got to the ground floor.

"Miss, I've been instructed to see you off the premises," he said firmly.

It was all Tami could do to nod in acknowledgement and then put one foot in front of the other as she left the building. Inside, her heart was slowly being torn into a million pieces. Somehow she had the presence of mind to call a cab and get home, where she stripped off her corporate clothing and made it into the shower. But as hard as she tried, she couldn't scrub away the sense of utter desolation that filled all the empty spaces inside. She'd brought this on herself. Her decisions. Her responsibility. Her mistakes.

After the shower, Tami wrapped up in her robe and curled in a ball under her bedcovers. Even then she couldn't escape the enormity of what she'd done. The vastness of her betrayal. Keaton's words continued to echo in her mind—*you are truly your father's daughter.* And it was true. In trying her hardest not to be like him at all, she'd allowed herself to become a tool for his use, and in doing so, had caused damage equally as bad as anything he'd ever done.

The weekend passed in a haze of nothingness. There was no one she could turn to. Early on Monday morning she was roused from her bed by the doorbell to her apartment. She peered through the peephole to see a courier standing there, and she opened her front door.

"Ms. Wilson?" he asked, holding his digital scanner toward her with a stylus at the ready.

"Yes," she answered.

"Parcel for you. Please sign on the screen."

She did as he asked and he bent to pick up the box at his feet and passed it to her.

"Have a great day!" he said cheerfully as he raced off down the hall.

Tami was beyond words. She recognized the logo on the address label of the box. Richmond Developments. Inside her apartment, she ripped open the lid and saw her personal effects from her desk nestled inside, together with a white envelope printed with her name on it. Inside was a statement from the legal department outlining the terms of the cessation of her employment, including, in detail, the alleged breaches of her employment agreement and the steps they would be taking against her to seek compensation.

Compensation? Knowing what the Tanner project would have been worth to them, she would need to live a hundred lifetimes before she could even scratch the financial surface of what she'd owe. And that wasn't even considering what she'd tried to repay to Our People, Our Homes. A sound erupted from her mouth. It should have been a hysterical laugh but it was more like a howl of desolation. She had never felt more wretched in her life.

Keaton paced the office. It had been three days since Tami's revelation and the sense of betrayal was as raw today as it had been back then. How had he been so stupid? Hadn't he learned his lesson with Honor? He'd called his brothers and sisters over the weekend and told them he'd let Tami go because she'd admitted to acting for Everard Corporation. They'd been equal parts shocked and angered at her duplicity. He hadn't quite been able to bring himself to tell them she was the old man's daughter. For some reason, he felt like it was his fault that he hadn't known sooner. Either way, it made no difference, she was gone and he and his siblings had agreed to start an internal investigation using an independent company so as not to alert any other potential plants within Richmond Developments as to what they were doing.

So far, only Monique in HR had been brought up for further investigation and she'd been arrested for facilitating corporate espionage, although it appeared there might be another infiltrator in the contracts division of the finance department. Kristin had been hot under the collar about that eye-opener and it had taken all her self-control not to face up to the guy and accuse him outright.

Honor had gently reminded them that there was a process to follow and that while it would take time, and they'd all hate the idea of knowing there were moles within their organization, it was better to do this methodically and in accordance with employment law.

But nothing took away the hurt that dwelled deep inside him that Tami had, from the outset, planned to spy on their company. And how, despite everything, he'd allowed her behind his carefully constructed walls and let her into his heart. Was he that poor a judge of character? He'd fought the feelings she'd engendered in him. He'd put the attraction down to being purely physical and congratulated himself on his ability to rule with his mind. But having kissed her that last night in Sedona, he'd honestly lost his battle with himself. The next week had been hell, knowing he'd probably hurt her with his rejection that night. And none of that had dimmed his need to reach out for her. Even now, he couldn't stop thinking about her, and that, more than anything, made him angry at himself and, unfortunately, everyone around him.

Even news from Fletcher that they had the lead on a new proposal that might help turn things around on the lost Tanner project was little comfort. Especially when, on a video call to discuss the various aspects they wanted to push where their company created a point of difference with others who might be pitching for the tender, he realized he was incorporating some of the suggestions Tami had made back on that first night in Sedona. Her suggestions about offering low-interest loans to allow low-income families into homes in better areas, and to bring affordable social housing into the project, had germinated in the back of his mind, and all his siblings had caught on to the idea and were expanding it with a financial team to see how it could be blended into the overall plan.

So how did someone like Tami, who'd turned out to be a total snake in the grass, have such a strong social conscience? To all appearances, she'd been good at her job and wasn't afraid to pitch for the underdog. And yet, that didn't gel with the fact that she'd deliberately walked into her role with the express purpose of feeding information back to her father. Keaton shook his head. He couldn't make sense of it and he'd allowed her far too much real estate in his mind already. It was time to shelve his feelings about her and let the legal department take care of the rest.

He turned as there was a knock at his office door and he saw Honor hovering there.

"You're looking rather fierce. Is it safe to come in?" she asked.

"Sure. I was just thinking."

Honor gave him a gentle smile. "That's definitely you. Always thinking. Sometimes overthinking, too, though. Am I right?"

He automatically smiled in response but there was no humor to it.

"You know me too well," he said bluntly.

Honor sat down in one of his guest chairs and he took the one opposite her.

"I do know you well, Keaton, and I have to admit that I'm really worried about you. You're not yourself."

"We're dealing with a lot here."

"We've been dealing with a lot here since December last year," she pointed out. "But that's not what I'm talking about. It's you, in here." She leaned forward and tapped him on the chest. "Something's not right. Talk to me. Tell me what's troubling you."

"Look, I really don't have time for—"

"Don't give me that, Keaton. If you don't make

time to talk to me now, when will you? And if not me, then who? Kristin? Logan? Your mom?"

He must have pulled a face because she carried on.

"See? Then it's me. Look, I know I hurt you, but I thought you were okay with Logan and me now. At least tell me if that's what is still upsetting you," she pressed.

"No, that's not what's upsetting me."

"There! So you admit you're upset about something."

Keaton groaned. "Of course I'm upset. We lost a major contract."

"But we're on the verge of winning another, so I know it's not that. Hmm, but I think it's tied to that somehow, isn't it?"

"Fine. Tami is Warren Everard's daughter. Satisfied now?"

Honor reeled back a little in shock. "His *daughter*?"

"His own personal spy."

Honor shook her head slowly. "Wow. I was shocked when you'd told us she'd been let go for spying. I have to be honest, from what I learned about her while we were in Sedona and in the days after we came home, for me at least, it just didn't ring true to her character. But now you're saying she's Everard's daughter? Do you think her father coerced her?"

He snorted a laugh but then became serious again as he weighed up telling Honor the rest of it. He had to tell someone. It was eating him up.

"We slept together." Okay, so maybe he hadn't

meant to be that blunt about it, but those three words pretty much summed it all up. "Do you think her father told her to do that, too?"

"You what?" Honor asked incredulously.

"You heard me."

"But you'd only known each other a couple of weeks."

"Three and a half, actually. Seriously, Honor, is there a statute of limitations on when a couple can have sex when they're attracted to one another? I would have thought you'd be the last person to cast judgment in that regard."

"No, of course not, and I'm not passing judgment," Honor said, with that same incredulous expression on her face. "But I know you—you don't rush into that kind of thing. She must have felt very special to you. No wonder you're hurting."

Tami had felt special to him. It's why the betrayal of finding out exactly who she was had made him so angry. Yes, and hurt, too.

"Keaton…" Honor leaned forward and stared earnestly into his eyes. "You know that sometimes people are driven to do things they would never normally do because of extenuating circumstances."

"Circumstances like you and Logan, last year?" he asked with a tinge of acrimony.

Honor's expression turned sad and he saw the shimmer of tears in her eyes. "I never wanted to hurt you, Keaton."

He felt something ease in his chest. "Yeah, I know. We weren't right for each other, no matter how hard we tried. And I'm sorry for that comment. It wasn't fair of me. I hold no bitterness toward you or Logan anymore. Don't feel guilty about it. Now I understand what it's like to be so drawn to someone that you go against your own common sense. I think I comprehend even better why you couldn't resist your attraction to Logan."

Honor bowed her head and wiped away an errant tear. "Thank you. That means a lot—and it'll mean a lot to Logan, too. But it doesn't solve the current issue, does it?"

"With Tami? It's solved. She's gone and Legal are preparing a case against her for breach of her employment contract."

"You're actually going after her?"

"She cost us millions of dollars, Honor. I can't just let that slide. Logan and Kristin are with me on this. Besides, it's not like her daddy can't afford to pay her damages, especially now he has the Tanner project."

Honor firmed her lips and shifted in her chair before answering. "Will it make the hurt go away?"

Keaton looked squarely at her. Trust Honor to cut straight to the chase.

"No, it won't, but it'll send a message to anyone else lurking in the shadows that we won't tolerate disloyalty of any kind."

"I can see that is necessary, but Tami really didn't seem the type to be into subterfuge and corporate espionage."

"Do those people ever broadcast what their true intentions are?"

"No, of course not, but you know what I mean, don't you? She was just too… I dunno…" She waved her hands in frustration. "Too nice. She was passionate about the things that make life good for people. Tami never struck me as the kind of person who made a single decision based on personal gain."

"She was clearly very good at her role as her father's pawn then, wasn't she?" he said cynically.

"I honestly don't think that was all an act. It makes me wonder what circumstances drove her to work for her father in that way. Maybe, if you can understand what those circumstances are, you can get a better grasp of why Tami did it."

"Do we really need to know why?"

"Keaton, you're an intelligent man with a compassionate heart, when you let anyone else see it. Can you honestly tell me you don't still care about her? That you aren't driven to figure out the why behind her actions?"

She got up to leave and gave him another long, concerned look before turning and heading for the door. Honor was asking too much. Figuring out why Tami spied on them was not on his agenda. The reason was obvious—money. It drove her father and it obviously drove her, too. But she'd been the one to come clean to him and she'd insisted that she hadn't passed any information on to her father. Keaton hadn't believed her then and he didn't feel inclined to believe her now. So where did that leave him? Was it Monique from HR or the snake in Kristin's department who'd passed on the information?

He weighed them up in his mind and rejected Monique almost immediately. She wouldn't have had clearance to access the information Everard wanted and IT had already scoured her computer and found no track back. And while the guy who'd been suspended pending an investigation in the finance department had a higher clearance, unless he was an extraordinarily skilled hacker, he wouldn't have been able to access the secure network where Keaton and his siblings had discussed the new venture. No, it all came back to Tami. She was the only person, outside of the family, he'd even mentioned the project to.

But what if Tami's father had gotten the information more indirectly from her somehow? He thought about when he and Tami had discussed the company's plans back in Sedona. She'd mentioned she'd made notes on her phone. Was that how Everard had found out? Did he have access to her phone? And, if he did, was she complicit or was she as innocent as she claimed?

Keaton huffed a sigh of frustration. However Warren Everard had gotten his data, the damage had been done and Tami was out of Richmond Developments and out of his life, even if he couldn't quite dislodge her from the back of his mind.

Ten

"I'm so glad you could come with me tonight," Nancy Richmond enthused as she led Keaton through the throng of heavily perfumed and expensively clad attendees at the charity dinner she'd coerced him into attending with her.

She'd been slow to get back out among her peers after the scandal and fallout from her husband's death last December, so he'd been pleased to be able to escort her this evening, to be honest.

"Me, too, Mom. You look exceptionally lovely tonight," he said with genuine feeling.

"Oh, you!" she said with a blush and patted his arm lovingly. "You always know how to say the right thing."

He placed his hand over hers and pressed her fingers in response. His mom had been an integral part of the management team at Richmond Developments for longer than he could remember, but with his father's sudden death, she'd withdrawn from almost every aspect of her life that had taken her outside her home. She'd grieved for far more than the man she'd loved intensely for over thirty years. Discovering their entire marriage had been mirrored with another woman and family on the other side of the continent had done a huge amount of damage to her confidence. Especially when it initially appeared that Nancy's marriage had been the bigamous one. By the time it was discovered that Douglas Richmond's first marriage had not been legal, the fallout had already been widespread. Keaton would have done anything to get her back to her old self, and if coming along to this two-thousand-dollar-a-plate dinner for a veteran's charity put a smile back on Nancy Richmond's face, then that's what he'd do.

"How's that lovely new assistant of yours doing?" Nancy asked after they'd been shown to their table. "I didn't tell you, did I? I popped into the office when you returned from Sedona. You were all locked in one of your meetings and Tami looked after me. We got to talking and she mentioned how she'd overcome her fear of flying and was super understanding about how I feel about it. Her suggestions on how to manage my anxiety made such good sense to me. So much so, Hector and I are thinking of a spa retreat to Palm Springs in a few weeks."

"That's great, Mom," Keaton said, equally surprised that Tami hadn't mentioned the time she'd spent with his mom and thrilled that his mother was beginning to think about taking steps away from home on her own. But hang on a minute… Hector was their family lawyer. He'd been a great support to Nancy, but a trip together? His father hadn't been gone that long.

"Oh, look at your face," Nancy said. "Don't worry, we don't plan to sleep together…yet."

Keaton blanched. Thinking about his parents that way was something he'd never done, but his mom and Hector? He really didn't want to go there.

"You're an adult in charge of your own choices," he said stiffly. "And, as to Tami, she has left us already."

"Oh, she didn't work out in the end? That's a shame."

"Actually, Mom, I had to let her go. She's Warren Everard's daughter."

"Really? Goodness! And she never told HR about the potential conflict of interest."

"We had reason to believe she was instrumental in us losing the Tanner project. It seems that an HR senior staffer was also on the Everard payroll and assisted in planting Tami in my office."

Nancy gasped in shock. "Well, I never. Still, if her father was behind it, it should come as no surprise. That man would stoop to anything to get what he wants. He and your father went head-to-head several times. Warren Everard always was a bastard—excuse my French."

"That's something I've always loved about you Mom—you like to call things as you see them."

"We have that in common, my darling boy," she said with a proud motherly smile. "But getting back to Warren and Margot Everard, everyone always said they were very difficult and demanding parents. They said they'd cut ties with their daughter once she turned eighteen but you know how people gossip. Many said it was more the other way around. Either way, I couldn't imagine doing that to one of my children, no matter how difficult their upbringing, but then again, Margot always was such a cold fish. Appearances meant everything to her. They still do.

"You know, given their situation, I can't imagine Tami ever wanting to work for her father. If there'd been a familial reconciliation I'm sure the gossip lines would have been buzzing. Why on earth would she do something like spy on you for him when they haven't spoken in years?"

"Who knows?" Keaton said with a shrug. "The fact remains that she admitted her relationship with Everard and what he'd asked her to do."

"Such a shame," Nancy said.

Keaton couldn't help but agree.

He had just returned from a run the next morning when his mom called, her voice throbbing with excitement.

"Keaton, you'll never believe what I've just heard!"

"Good morning to you, too, Mom. It was a lovely night last night, thank you."

"Oh, yes, all of that," she said offhandedly. "But listen. One of my girlfriends phoned me for a chat today and she said that she'd heard from Bitsy Tyler, whose daughter is married to that guy who works in the prosecutor's office. I never liked him, you know, he's got snaky eyes and a fidget that makes you wonder what he's thinking all the time. Anyway, Bitsy said that Warren Everard's daughter was under investigation by the police for her involvement in a rather large sum of missing money from the Our People, Our Homes charity."

Keaton stood still and gripped his phone so tightly the plastic squeaked. "Just how much money are we talking here?"

"Their entire operating capital. Two and a half million dollars."

He let out a long, low whistle. "And she's accused of taking it?"

"No…well, not directly, anyway. Apparently she was dating her boss—he was the director of the charity and now neither he, nor the money, are anywhere to be found. One of my bridge-club ladies apparently asked Margot Everard to her face about it yesterday and Margot said they have no contact with their daughter and she had nothing to say on the matter."

Keaton barely heard her after the part where Nancy told him that Tami had been dating the charity's director. It raised all sorts of ugly questions in his mind. Did she make a habit of sleeping with all her bosses?

"Do you think she was an active party to it, Keaton?"

He dragged his attention back to her question. A part of him wanted to say an emphatic yes, but there was a tickle at the back of his mind that urged him to look beyond what had been presented on the surface.

"It's hard to say without knowing more, Mom. And it's not our place to discuss it, to be honest. If she's being investigated we have to trust that they will uncover her involvement, or establish her innocence."

"I can't accept that the lovely girl I met in your office would be capable of such a thing."

On the surface, Keaton would normally have agreed with his mom, but then he had his own experience of Tami's ability to appear to be one thing when she was very definitely another.

"Appearances can be deceptive, Mom. We all learned that the hard way with Dad."

His mom went silent on the other end of the phone and he cursed himself for his insensitivity.

"Mom, look, I'm sorry, I shouldn't have said that."

"No, darling, you're right. Appearances can be deceptive, but I've had a lot of time to think about my situation and for all that your father cheated on me the entire time I knew him, he still managed to provide me with a very good life and three children I love to the moon and back. What he did was wrong on so many levels I still can't bear to think of them all. But I've learned to move past that and, in my own way, find forgiveness for him for what he did to us because if I hadn't been able to do that, I would forever be a victim of his circumstances, and that I refuse to do."

"You're an incredible woman, Mom. I'm so proud of you."

"And I'm proud of you, too. I'll let you know if I hear any more about Tami. I'm sure there's more there than meets the eye."

Keaton ended the call and went to take a shower. He leaned his forearms against the tiled wall of the shower stall and set the jets of the shower to a penetrating pulse down the back of his neck and his shoulders. A part of him continued to seethe with fury over the betrayal he believed Tami was responsible for, especially in light of her apparent involvement in the theft of funds from the charity she'd worked at before. But that niggle in the back of his mind continued to urge him to push harder and look deeper.

As to his mother's forgiveness for his father, he wasn't prepared to rejoin the Douglas Richmond fan club just yet. He'd idolized his father his entire life. Had dedicated every breath in his body to making his father proud. Everything he'd done or achieved had been because he'd given twice as much effort, as if he could somehow make up for his missing twin. He'd worked damn hard for everything he had achieved. He'd made sacrifices and not stopped to count the cost. And for what? To be overthrown the second Logan had turned up. As the older twin, his brother had taken over everything that Keaton had worked for his entire life, even his fiancée. Then, to add further insult to injury, to discover he, Logan and Kristin were not Douglas's only children? Well, that had been a shock too far. Keaton didn't think he'd ever be capable of thinking about his father without the deep sense of betrayal that had infiltrated pretty much everything in Keaton's life in the past four months.

Keaton snapped off the faucet, stepped from the shower and grabbed a towel. As he dried off, he accepted he was going to have to talk again with Tami. The gossip his mom had shared with him raised more questions than provided answers.

Once he was dried off and dressed, Keaton checked the personnel file he had in his laptop for Tami and typed a note in his phone with her address. They were going to have this out, right now.

Keaton did a quick check on the address he'd entered into his GPS. Yes, this was definitely the one. There was certainly no evidence here that Tami was the daughter of one of Seattle's richest men, nor that she'd had any benefit from the two and a half million dollars that was reportedly missing. This suburb was everyday, middle America—nice, certainly, but not what he'd been expecting for Warren Everard's daughter.

The clapboard home was small and set back on the lot. A small garden looked as though it struggled to survive out front and the path to the door showed signs of weeds coming through the cracks in the path. He went up the shallow stairs that led to the front door and knocked hard, still unconvinced he had the correct address. It wasn't long before he heard movement behind the door.

"Who is it?"

That was definitely Tami.

"It's Keaton. I need to talk to you."

He heard the sound of a chain being slid off the door before the lock turned and the door slowly opened. His eyes roamed her instantly, taking in the dark discoloration beneath her eyes, which lacked any of their usual sparkle, and the paleness of her face. She wore a pair of yoga pants and an oversize woolen sweater that dwarfed her frame. And yet, despite all that, his body reacted instantly to her. He clamped down on the urge that spiraled through him and of all the memories of their lovemaking—of how she sounded, tasted, smelled—that his mind seemed determined to revisit.

Tami could barely take her eyes off him. Dressed in a good pair of casual trousers and a finely knitted sweater, Keaton looked as if he'd just stepped away from a designer photo shoot. Even his hair was its trademark perfect. His cool gray eyes looked straight back at her and she shifted slightly under his scrutiny, suddenly self-conscious of her appearance. She knew she didn't look good and hadn't cared, right up until this moment.

"May I come in?" he asked, his voice a little more gruff than usual.

"Of course," she answered in a small voice and stepped back to allow him into her hallway.

As he stepped past her, she caught a trace of his cologne, the woodsy scent reminding her of what it had been like to be close enough to him to feel as though they'd been one unit, working together. But she'd ruined all that, hadn't she? She dragged in a breath and closed the door behind him.

"I'm sorry, I wasn't expecting anyone. Please, come through to the kitchen. Can I get you anything?"

"Coffee would be great."

As she moved about the kitchen, she felt his gaze on her, even watching her every movement as she measured out beans into the coffee grinder, as if he didn't trust her to do even that right. Her hand shook and she dropped some beans on the countertop. She was turning into a clumsy wreck. She cleaned up and put the coffee on, before turning to face him. The sooner he cut to the chase, the sooner he'd leave.

"You said you needed to talk to me. What about?"

He must know she'd already received the document from the legal department of Richmond Developments outlining her responsibilities under her employment agreement and then listing her breach of the same, and that they would be seeking damages. Surely, he hadn't needed to come to her door to discuss that further? Faced with the other disaster in her life—the investigation into Our People, Our Homes—dealing with Richmond Developments was peanuts in comparison.

She was surprised when Keaton began to outline the investigation into the charity and her alleged involvement in it. A sour taste rose in her mouth. It seemed the grapevine had been well and truly busy.

"The business of embezzlement at Our People, Our Homes. Is it true?" he asked.

"What exactly are you asking? Did I steal the money? No, of course not! It is true that I let Mark use my password-protected computer—he was my boss and my boyfriend. I had no reason to believe he'd abuse my trust. It's also true that he filtered the money through our joint bank account before immediately transferring it all out again."

Keaton looked squarely at her. "Were you involved in that?"

It was as if she hadn't even spoken. Hadn't he listened to a word she'd just said? Tami closed her eyes, counted to three, then opened them again.

"Only in that I let him use my computer. In itself, that was a breach of the user agreement I signed when I started at Our People, Our Homes."

The coffee machine hissed and spat its conclusion and Tami grabbed two mugs and began to pour the coffee. Her hands were still shaking and she hissed under her breath as a few droplets of the steaming-hot brew splattered onto her hand. Thank goodness Keaton hadn't noticed or he'd probably see her nervousness as some kind of admission of guilt.

"And you're adamant that's the extent of your involvement?"

"Look, I don't see that it's any of your business, Keaton, but, yes. That is the extent of my involvement. And that's what I told the police over four hours of questioning yesterday afternoon and six hours the day before, when they came to my house. The only thing I'm guilty of is giving Mark access to my computer.

"We were cosignatories on the charity accounts and it never occurred to me to distrust him. I thought I loved him, so why wouldn't I trust him? He kept talking about the future, about what we'd do together. For the first time in my life, I thought I'd found someone who loved me for myself and not for what advantage I could give them because of the family I was born into. Yes, being in a relationship together and being cosignatories was probably not wise. I should have requested to be removed from the signing authorities when things got serious between us. But it never occurred to me that he was using me. Even when I was faced with what he'd done I could barely believe it.

"Now, looking back, I can see that he groomed me, wooed me, then manipulated me to get ahold of that money. And, in doing so, he set me up to look equally as guilty and left me as the fall guy to take the blame. Even though I knew it looked as if I was complicit in the whole thing, I took it straight to the board. I laid everything bare to them and I presented them with a solution."

It was a far-fetched story, but she hoped the truth rang clear in her words.

"A solution?"

He was dogged, she'd give him that.

"Because I was responsible for the loss, I offered to make full restitution so we could continue to operate. I should have known it was a stretch and that I should have just allowed them to follow the correct procedure from the start when the loss was exposed. But I went to my father for help. I don't know why I thought that anything might ever have changed between us, but at the time going to him was the only avenue I could see to make things right again. He's a trustee of a fund left to me by my grandmother. I asked him for access to the fund to repay the money Mark had stolen. He agreed, but had conditions."

Keaton grunted, then went silent a while before speaking again.

"If you didn't take the money, why did you attempt to refund it? Why aren't the authorities chasing this Mark guy down and making him pay it back?"

Tami felt her throat tighten. How many times did she have to say it before he'd believe her?

"He is under investigation, now, but he's left the country. As to me wanting to return the money–I gave Mark the access and I ignored the safeguards set in place to prevent exactly that from happening. Me. No one else. I felt it was my responsibility."

"He still had to make the choice to abuse your trust. Where is he now?"

"From what I understand, the money was traced to an offshore account, and Mark…well, the police believe he's enjoying the tropical climate of Nauru. And, of course, there is no extradition treaty between the USA and the islands of Micronesia." She sighed heavily. "He did his research all right. And all the time he was doing that, right under my nose, I believed him when he said he was planning a vacation for us. I guess I was so wrapped up in the idyll of being loved for myself, that I didn't see the signs that I was being exploited. The police aren't fully convinced that I'm not just biding my time, either, waiting to join him."

"Are you?"

"No! Of course not. And to prove it I voluntarily surrendered my passport before they asked for it and I'm cooperating fully with the investigation."

"And this business with Everard. Exactly what did he expect from you?"

Tears sprang into Tami's eyes and her fingers tightened around her coffee mug. She blinked fiercely and took a long sip of the brew before answering.

"He expected me to find out what you were working on and report back to him. The outdoors experience set his plans back a little, I think. He messaged me several times a day while we were away."

"And you told him what we'd discussed on our first night?"

She shook her head vehemently. "I told him absolutely nothing about that. When we arrived back here in Seattle, I went to see him. He told me in no uncertain terms that I wouldn't see a penny of my money because I hadn't personally given him the information he'd needed, and then he basically kicked me out of the house." She swallowed another sip of coffee, the burn of it in her stomach reminding her that she probably should have eaten at some stage in the past twenty-four hours. But then again, the idea of putting food in her mouth had made her stomach lurch uncomfortably.

"Look, Keaton, I don't know what you want from me, but I never told my father anything about the Tanner project. I know that I don't exactly look like the innocent party in any of this, but I wish you could believe me."

"I wish I could, too," he said quietly.

His words excoriated her heart and she knew, in that moment, that in his eyes she was damned no matter what she said.

"I'd like you to leave now," she said firmly.

"One last thing," Keaton said as he rose to leave. "The phone you used while we were away. Had you had that long?"

"No, why?"

"May I ask where you got it?"

"My mother gave it to me when she organized my new corporate wardrobe," Tami said. "Which reminds me, I need to donate those clothes somewhere. She said that Dad insisted I have the best technology available so I would at least look the part in my new role as your assistant."

Even then her father hadn't believed in her enough to think she could do a job well.

"Would you mind loaning the phone to me? I'd like to have our IT people look at it. I promise we'll get it back to you."

"Sure. I don't use it now, anyway. I'll grab it for you on your way out."

Tami led the way down the hallway and opened the front door for him, leaving him standing in the hallway as she ducked into her bedroom and retrieved the phone from where she'd tossed it to the back of a drawer in her dresser. She handed it to Keaton and their fingers brushed, the warmth of his skin instantly permeating hers. The sensation robbed her of breath, but the moment he took the phone he severed their contact almost instantly.

"Keaton, I'm really sorry. I wish I could go back and undo all the harm I've caused."

He looked at her, his eyes sharp and clear, before nodding abruptly.

"We'll courier it back to you," he said as he moved out the front door.

"Don't bother. I don't want anything to do with a single thing from my father."

And in the next second he was outside and on the path heading for his car, as if he couldn't wait to be clear of her. Tami rubbed her hand down her thigh, ridding herself of the sensation of his all-too-brief touch. And, as she watched him drive away and closed the door behind her, a shocking sense of loss billowed from deep within and drove her to her knees. She'd never felt so alone in her entire life.

Eleven

Keaton read the report that had come with the returned phone. That niggling suspicion of his had been confirmed. Tami's phone not only had a remote-access function that had allowed a third party to listen in on calls and conversations, but everything she'd done, from photos she'd taken through notes she'd made on a notetaking app on the phone, had also been backed up to a cloud that was registered to an anonymous user.

He had no doubt that if they explored further, they would discover the anonymous user was most likely a company sheltering under the umbrella of Everard Corporation. Keaton made a sound of disgust and tossed the report to his desk before getting up from his chair and striding over to the window. He heard the office door open, but was too absorbed in anger at the magnitude of what Tami had unwittingly done to bother turning around to identify his visitor.

"Problem?" Logan's voice came from behind him.

"Read that," Keaton said, half turning and gesturing angrily to the printed report on his desk.

Logan let out a long, low whistle. "So that's how the old bastard did it. Do you still think she was complicit?"

Keaton's initial reaction was to utter a sharp affirmative, but in light of the information he'd received from his mom and what Tami herself had told him, she either had to be the best actress and liar in the history of womankind, or she'd been cruelly duped. Not once, but twice. And each time by the men she should have been able to trust would love and protect her.

"Not fully, no. She did mean to spy, but didn't know she was being duped by her own father at the same time."

"So what now?"

"What do you mean, what now? Even if it was inadvertent, she still gave Everard the information he needed."

"Are we still going to bring a case against her?"

Keaton swung around to face his twin. It was still slightly disconcerting to feel as though he was looking at himself in a mirror. Aside from a chickenpox scar above Logan's right eyebrow, it would take someone who knew both men extremely well to be able to tell the difference between them. And, after a lifetime of believing he was an only son, and now discovering the twin he'd developed with in utero was still alive, it had been a hard road to accepting his brother into his life.

"Y—" Keaton couldn't say it. While he was still furious she'd come under their umbrella with every intention of spying, she hadn't completely followed through. Was it enough that she'd been fired? Probably. "I'll think about it."

Logan sat down in one of the chairs opposite Keaton's desk and crossed one leg lazily over the other.

"What are you doing?" Keaton asked.

"Waiting for you to open up and admit you have feelings for that girl."

Keaton threw himself back into his chair and stared back at his brother. "Honor's been talking to you, hasn't she?"

"Of course she has, but, honestly, even a blind man could see you're hurting and it's not just the loss of a contract that's made you more prickly than *kina*."

"*Kina*?"

"Sorry, I forget. You guys call 'em sea urchins, I think. You know, a squat round shell with spines about this long—" he gestured with his fingers "—and meaty flesh inside. It's a delicacy back in New Zealand."

"If you say so," Keaton answered uncomfortably. He wasn't sure if he was comfortable about being likened to a sea creature, especially one with spines.

"I do. So talk to me about Tami."

"I don't know where to start. She arrived and

somehow inveigled her way into pretty much every thought I've had since."

"Sounds like love to me."

"No. I've been in love." He stared at the brother who was currently engaged to his own ex-fiancée.

"Be honest. Did you feel for Honor the way Tami makes you feel?"

"We barely know each other," he protested.

"Yeah, you do. In here." Logan pointed to his chest. "Even if you're fighting it in your head, your heart knows. Take it from me. Trust your heart."

"I don't know if I can."

"Sure you do. You just need to take the leap. Metaphorically speaking, of course." Logan got up from his chair and flung his brother a smile. "See you later at dinner at Mom's."

Logan left him ruminating on his thoughts. Keaton picked up the report and read it again. Tami could have consented to all of this spyware on her phone, but if she was telling the truth, she'd been thoroughly tricked. Knowing how passionate she was for the underdog, it just seemed wrong that others could have used her this way, especially her family. He stared at the doorway his brother had just exited. Yes, there'd been a time when he'd wished Logan had never come back to the States. But, for all their banter, imagining a life without him now was impossible. Keaton knew it would destroy him if he was alienated from his family the way Tami was.

He thought back to something Tami had said when he'd gone to visit her. *For the first time in my life,*

I thought I'd found someone who loved me for myself. With what little he knew about her upbringing, he could imagine that when people knew she was Warren Everard's daughter they might have formed sycophantic relationships if they thought it would gain them access to the Everard money. Even he and Kristin had faced that through school, and to a lesser degree in college. Some kids gravitated to those with privileged backgrounds for reasons other than genuine friendship. Some adults, too. Was that all Tami's life had been? No wonder she'd been so eager to please her boyfriend.

Keaton knew there was obviously very little love between her and her parents. Even that he found hard to comprehend. For all his own father's faults, Douglas Richmond had loved his family—families, Keaton corrected himself—deeply, and within those families, they'd been brought up to love and respect one another, too. Despite all she'd been through, Tami had grown into a warm and compassionate woman. Someone who deserved better than to have her faith in people violated by the very ones to whom she should always be able to turn.

So what, exactly, was this creep she'd imagined herself in love with like? Keaton wondered. What had she called him again? Mark? He pulled up the name of the charity on his computer and searched for their website, then any reference to the people running the charity. There was only one person who fit—a Mark Pennington was still listed as the director of the organization. Keaton opened a new search window and keyed in the guy's name. There wasn't a lot to be found about him, even through social media. Just a couple of references to college sports and some public appeal he'd headed for the Our People, Our Homes charity. It was as if he'd deliberately wiped as much personal information as he possibly could from the internet, which was no small feat.

But there had to be a way to track him down and make him face the law for what he'd done. Keaton put a call through to their head of security—Janice May, who'd spent many years on the Seattle police force—and asked her for a meeting. After an intense hour of discussion, Keaton had a plan to move forward. Clearly Mark Pennington was a man motivated by easy money. If he could dangle a sufficiently enticing get-rich-quick scheme in front of him, it might just be enough to get Pennington to leave his tropical-island sanctuary and set foot on home soil. The minute he did that, the police would be ready to pounce. Janice had already spoken with an old colleague who'd confirmed there was a warrant out for Pennington's arrest.

He would have loved to be the person baiting the trap for Pennington himself. But there were a couple of reasons why he couldn't. The first was his desire to likely pulverize the guy for being such a lowdown dirty cheat. The second was that he was needed here. He couldn't afford to take his eye off the ball here at work. Janice had suggested a private firm that would be able to assist him—all he needed to do was dream up a suitable scheme to bait the trap with enough money that would appeal to Pennington. The guy was a greedy slimeball, so Keaton didn't think that would be too difficult.

Careful planning was all it would take and Keaton was nothing if not careful. Two days later, his representative was on a series of flights to Nauru and the sting was in place. Now it was merely a waiting game.

"Why don't you answer your phone!" Warren Everard demanded from the front porch of Tami's house. "You'd have saved me the trouble of coming to this dump!"

"Well, if you called my phone, I would answer it," she said, blocking her doorway and refusing to let him in.

Keaton had sent her an express envelope, which had included a copy of the report from the IT people at Richmond Developments. She'd been shocked to see how easily her father had manipulated her and accessed information she'd thought was private. There was no way she was letting him inside her modest home. It might not be much, but it was her sanctuary and she'd worked hard for it.

She reached into the back pocket of her jeans and checked the screen on her old, outdated mobile, then held it up to him.

"See, no calls, no messages."

"Not that piece of junk," he sneered. "I mean the phone I gave you when you started at Richmond."

"Oh, that phone. That would be the one you

planted spyware in so you could keep tabs on me and renege on the agreement we made?"

He didn't even have the grace to look shamefaced.

Tami sighed wearily. "Why are you here, Dad? I thought you said you were done with me."

"I wish," he muttered with a sour expression on his face. "I want to know if you knew that crowd at Richmond damn well set me up!"

There was an unusual gray cast to Warren Everard's skin that was at odds with his normally ruddy complexion. And his breathing was labored, as if he was under great physical stress.

"Are you okay, Dad? You don't look well."

"Of course I'm not well," he snapped. "Now answer the damned question!"

"No need to shout at me. Knew what, exactly?"

"About the contamination?"

"What contamination?"

"Don't play games with me. I know precisely how cozy you got with Keaton Richmond. Did he set the whole thing up just to see me fall?"

Tami paled. Keaton's covering letter had told her the spyware her father had had installed on the phone could pick up conversations and phone calls, as well as back up notes to where he could access them. Did that mean he'd heard *everything* between her and Keaton? Even their lovemaking?

A hot flush of embarrassment began to flood her body, but it was rapidly followed by an anger that she'd never felt before. This was a violation that went beyond corporate espionage. She had no cause to feel

rsrt3

embarrassment. She should feel nothing but pity for the man who'd fathered her. He was so driven that he considered nothing private. So driven that he thought he had the right to win at all costs and to hell with anyone who stood in his way.

"What…contamination?" she said deliberately.

"The Tanner project. The entire thing is stalled because of land contamination due to illegal toxic dumping in the area thirty years ago. Bastards falsified reports and hid the truth so deep even my lawyers didn't find the details until it was too late. When I sent out my people they began ground testing, which subsequently raised so many red flags I'm surprised the land doesn't glow at night. Keaton Richmond knew about it, didn't he?"

Tami shook her head slowly. "Dad, he was privy to the same information you were before making the pitch. He knew nothing."

"I don't believe you. I'm suing everybody involved with this. The vendors, the realtors and if I discover Richmond Developments knew any of this I'm going to damn well sue them too. We're going to be tied up in court now for so long I'll probably never live long enough to see the conclusion. This is going to cost me millions!"

He turned sharply and stomped his way down the path to the road, where his driver waited patiently beside the car. She watched as he got in and the car then drove away. A tiny smile curled her lips.

She shouldn't feel so satisfied when this was clearly making her father ill, she told herself. But the fact was, he'd used subterfuge to steal that contract out from under Richmond Developments and he was now reaping his just reward as far as she was concerned. That it had led to a very lucky escape for Keaton's team was a monumental bonus. She doubted, given the struggles the company was experiencing at present, that they'd have weathered the fallout her father now faced from the Tanner project without major losses.

Tami also wondered how her father would feel when he received the correspondence she'd directed her newly appointed lawyer to send him. She'd approached a law firm to act on her behalf in the Our People, Our Homes case and the Richmond Developments matter. While there, she'd mentioned her father restricting her access to her trust fund and her lawyer had made the appropriate enquiries. The information requested had confirmed her father had blocked her late grandmother's wishes regarding Tami's access to the fund, citing Tami's instability and unreliable character.

While he had, judging from the balance sheet provided, managed her trust fund very well since her grandmother had passed away ten years ago, she couldn't see him being fair going forward, not after the way he'd abused his position as the trustee of her fund, or with the Tanner project. It was past time for her to take more control into her own hands, to have a say in how the fund was handled. Her father's actions had weaponized the fund that was rightfully hers to manage. And, given the way he'd treated her recently, there was no way she had any reason to ever be in contact with him again, or have him control a single aspect of her life, so her attorney had been instructed to take steps to see to Warren Everard's removal as a trustee.

She turned and went inside, feeling freer than she had in a very long time. After what had happened with Mark, and then her father's manipulation of her, she knew she couldn't be that person anymore. She needed to take charge of the things that were important to her. Making everyone around her happy was all very well, but she needed to take care of herself, too.

Would Keaton have heard the news about the Tanner project yet? It was possible her father had only just found out, and when he couldn't reach her had driven straight to her house. Should she call Keaton, or maybe go and see him? Tami grabbed her mobile phone and began to key in his number but the phone beeped three times and then the screen went dark. The battery was dead. Since phoning was now out, that meant she had to go see him. She doubted she'd be permitted back into the Richmond tower, but maybe she could try to catch him at home.

Before she could talk herself out of it, she grabbed her car keys and bag and headed out the door. Keaton deserved to get the news on the Tanner project now, and not through some other intermediary source. When she got to his apartment tower, however, she hadn't counted on the security guard being the same guy who'd been on duty when she'd left the last time.

"But this is important—I must see him," Tami insisted.

"No, miss. It's more than my job is worth to let you upstairs. Send him a letter."

Tami groaned and started to turn away, but caught sight of the very man she needed to see coming in through the main doors from the street.

"Jeffrey, is there a problem?" Keaton asked as he drew near.

"I'm sorry, Mr. Richmond. I've told her she's not permitted on the premises, but she refuses to leave. Would you like me to call the police?"

Tami wheeled around to face Keaton. "Please, I won't be long. It's really important or I wouldn't be here. I promise."

Keaton looked at the security guard. "It won't be necessary to call the police." He shifted his gaze to Tami. "Come with me."

He led her to the elevators and they ascended to his floor. Through the short journey, he didn't make eye contact, nor did he say a word. Maybe this hadn't been the greatest of her ideas, Tami thought as she watched the numbers count inexorably up. She let out a breath as the elevator pinged and the doors slid open, then followed Keaton down the thickly carpeted hall to his door.

Inside, she was assailed with the memory of her last visit here. Of how they had barely made it past the entrance foyer, so strong had been their hunger for one another. It sent a shiver of longing through her body.

"Cold?" Keaton asked.

"No," she answered, staring straight into his eyes.

She noted the exact moment his pupils flared and his sharp intake of breath as he understood exactly where her thoughts had been.

"Take a seat in the living room," he said. "I'll be back in a minute."

She did as he said, and was again lost in the memory of the state she'd been in the last time she'd sat here. Sated, yes, but tied up in a hundred knots for the truth she'd had to deliver. And now? Well, she was just tied up in knots.

She started when Keaton returned. He'd changed out of his suit and into a pair of trousers and a finely woven sweater that looked like it had cost more than her monthly house payments. A look at the subtle logo on his breast confirmed her suspicion.

"Can I offer you anything to drink?" he asked.

"No, thank you. I meant it when I said I wouldn't be long. I wanted to tell you the news myself, before it makes headlines tomorrow, which I'm sure it will do."

"And that is?" he said, sitting down opposite her.

"It's to do with the Tanner project," she began.

Keaton stiffened in his chair. "Go on."

"The land is contaminated. My father came to see me about an hour ago. He accused me of setting him up." She uttered a bitter laugh. "Ironic, isn't it? He used me and now he blames me. Anyway, that's not what I'm here to say. I just wanted you to know that I'm glad he beat you to that contract. Apparently a large tract of the land was an illegal toxic dump site and the records were purged somehow. If the past is any example, I'm guessing the land will need be left empty until testing levels show it is safe for development. Given my father's reaction, I'm guessing that will be a very long time."

Keaton leaned forward, his forearms resting on his thighs and his hands clasped together. "You're certain of this."

"Oh, yes, he came to my front door and told me himself. To be honest, he looked physically ill over it. And I'm not surprised. A part of me does feel some compassion for what he must be going through—I wouldn't be me, if I didn't. But overall I'm just so relieved that Richmond Developments has dodged a bullet. Anyway, I wanted you to know first. Before it makes the news."

Keaton leaned back again in his chair and blew out a long breath. "Wow, I was not expecting that. But thank you for coming to tell me. The rest of the family will be thrilled."

Tami let her eyes roam over him and felt that familiar tug of need deep in her chest. She wished things could have been different between them, but wishes weren't reality. She knew that only too well.

"Well," she said as she slowly rose to her feet. "That's all I wanted to say. Thank you for hearing me out. Don't bother getting up. I'll let myself out."

She felt his body heat behind her before she even got to the door.

"Tami?"

She hesitated, turned. This close she could see the silver striations in his eyes. She swallowed. There were bare inches between them. All she had to do was close the distance and she could kiss him. But that could never happen again. She'd betrayed him. He'd never want to build again on the camaraderie they'd shared during the outdoors experience, nor repeat that night they shared almost two weeks ago. Trust was all-important to him and he didn't believe he could trust her, even when she'd shown him that she wasn't the bad guy here. But she had entered his business with the intention of stealing information, and for that she would forever be filled with regret. She'd never counted on feeling like this about him. Never counted on wanting to love him.

"Yes?"

He took in a deep breath. Every part of her yearned to hear him ask her to stay. To say he'd forgiven her for her intentions. To say his feelings for her mirrored her own.

"Thank you for coming here today. I appreciate that you brought the news to me in person."

She deflated like a pricked balloon.

"Yeah, well, it was the right thing to do. I might have made some stupid decisions in my life, but I do always try to do good. Maybe you'll be able to find it in your heart to believe me and, in time, forgive me. Goodbye, Keaton."

Tami turned and fumbled for the door handle, then flinched as Keaton reached past her to open the door for her. She mumbled something that might have sounded like a thank-you, before heading back down the hall and to the elevator. She kept it together until she reached her car, and once she was inside, key in the ignition and doors locked, she let go all of the nerves and tension and, yes, even the tiny flicker of hope that had bloomed for an infinitesimal moment, and sobbed at the empty future that now faced her.

Twelve

Keaton couldn't get Tami out of his head. A part of him knew he needed to put this whole business behind him and take a stride forward into his future. Another part of him hung back, telling him he wasn't done here yet. And that part questioned his every thought and every decision. It was an unhealthy obsession, he told himself, and yet he couldn't stop the snippets of memory that would pop into his thoughts at any given time of the day or night. Even at his apartment, she invaded his thoughts. Not even his bedroom felt the same anymore.

If he was to be totally honest with himself, his life felt empty and he didn't like it one bit. He should be on top of the world, he told himself. They'd dodged a flaming arrow with the Tanner project and the new bid for the job Fletcher had initiated had been accepted. Everything was on the up. Logan and Honor had set a date for their wedding this coming summer, while his mom had booked the Palm Springs retreat with Hector. Even Kristin seemed marginally happier these days.

He'd thought it would be easy to move on without Tami in his sphere—after all, they'd only known each other a very short time—but somehow she'd inveigled her way into every nook and cranny of his mind. And, yeah, his heart, too, if he was going to be totally honest. It seemed Logan actually knew him better than he knew himself—in relation to Tami, at least.

He paced the floor with nervous energy. Today Mark Pennington was due to arrive on a flight from New Zealand to Los Angeles, and then catch the next available flight to Seattle. It turned out that the offer of a very lucrative contract to appear to manage the dispersal of twenty million dollars through several charities, but to filter the money instead into an offshore account and eventually distribute it between himself, Jones and Keaton, had been just the right enticement to get Pennington to risk his safe position in Nauru. Sure, he'd tried to avoid actually returning to US soil—saying he could do all that remotely— but an offer of an additional bonus apparently sweetened the deal enough for him to hop on a plane. Jones, the guy he'd hired from the private investigation firm and who'd visited Pennington in Nauru, would collect him from the airport and take him to a restaurant, where Keaton would join them as part of the sting. Keaton would be wired so everything Pennington said in their meeting could be recorded and, where possible, used to bring any additional charges against him.

Keaton checked his watch for the umpteenth time and realized it would be a good idea to head to the restaurant now. He'd be wired up there before the investigator and Pennington arrived. He used a driver to get him to the destination in Renton. The restaurant would have no other patrons this evening aside from a few plainclothes officers who would be involved in the arrest.

Security buzzed from downstairs to let him know his car and driver were waiting. Keaton was glad to finally be moving and became filled with a sense of purpose. He was doing this for Tami and for the charity that had been ripped off. Maybe once this was done he'd be able to draw a line under the whole experience and start afresh.

The restaurant was dimly lit and the offerings from the laminated menu leaned heavily on fried food. The tablecloth was none too clean, either, Keaton observed as he sat down at the table after being prepped by the technician with the trace equipment. One of the officers from the three small groups scattered around the restaurant rose and joined Keaton at the table.

"Jack Hima, pleased to meet you. Thanks for helping us out here," the man said, extending his hand.

Keaton took it and smiled. "Feels very cloak-and-dagger, doesn't it?"

"Sometimes you have to think like a rat to catch one."

"And this guy really is a rat."

Hima nodded. "We've done a little poking into his past. There are warrants for him under another name. He's a greedy bastard, all right. Likes the high life on other people's money. But don't worry, we'll get him this time and once we're done with him in Washington, he'll be facing charges in Oregon and Idaho as well."

It sounded like Pennington was a professional thief. It irked Keaton intensely that he hadn't been caught up until now. But his reign of abuse would end today and it gave Keaton no small amount of pleasure to know that. Tami hadn't stood a chance against a man like Pennington. She was the most open and accepting person Keaton had ever met. He only wished she hadn't agreed to spy on him for her father.

Hima slid his phone from his pocket and checked the screen. "Looks like they're almost here. I'll go back to my seat. Just remember, keep it business, as we coached you. A guy like this has a big ego. Hopefully, he'll trip himself up and give us more to hold against him before we make the arrest. If not, we'll take him down, anyway."

Keaton nodded and took a deep breath to calm the nerves that had begun to flutter in his stomach. He really wasn't cut out for this undercover stuff. He vastly preferred the cut and thrust of business to this kind of thing, which belonged in the shadows. He saw a movement at the main entrance to the restaurant and two men entered. The hostess, another plainclothes officer, he'd been told, showed them to his table. He rose, and even though it went against every honorable notion that had been drilled into him by his parents, he offered his hand to Pennington.

"Glad you could make it," he said.

He stared at the guy. Obviously he'd been traveling a long time, probably the better part of twenty-four hours not counting layovers. His clothing was disheveled, his eyes red-rimmed, and his hair stuck out as if he'd been running his hands through it several times. He kept looking around nervously, as if expecting someone to jump out of the woodwork at him. Which they would do, eventually, Keaton thought with satisfaction.

"Yeah, well, you made an interesting proposition. Let's get down to business."

He and the investigator sat at the table with Keaton, then the hostess came over with menus and filled water glasses.

"You hungry?" Keaton asked as he saw Pennington eye the menu thoroughly.

"Starved."

"Go ahead, order. It's on me," Keaton said with as much munificence as he could muster.

"Thanks, I will."

Pennington raised a hand and gestured for someone to come and take his order. He ordered a double order of fries and a triple decker burger with cheese sauce on everything, together with a beer.

"You ordering?" Pennington asked Keaton and the other man.

"No, I'm good. You?" Keaton asked the investigator.

"Just some coffee, thanks."

When the waitress had gone, Pennington sat forward on his chair and stared at Keaton.

"How did you find me?"

"You were hiding?" Keaton asked, avoiding the direct question.

Pennington grinned and Keaton got a glimpse of what he must look like when he wasn't jet-lagged. Yeah, the guy had a certain charm, which was obviously what had appealed to Tami. That and the fact they'd been working together for what she'd believed was the common good would have made him all the more likable as far as someone like her was concerned. An unexpected anger boiled up deep from inside Keaton and he forced himself to tamp it down. Pennington would get his just deserts.

"You could say that. I might have pissed off a few people."

Keaton smiled in return, remembering Hima's comment about trapping a rat by being like one. "That'd be the Our People, Our Homes board and management, I imagine."

"Oh, you heard about that?"

Pennington cast a considering look at Keaton and looked uncomfortable for a moment. As if he was debating getting up and leaving. But Keaton kept his expression as bland as he could.

"I have my spies," Keaton said with a conspiratorial smile. "Nice work on that one."

The words tasted like sawdust in his mouth but they did the trick and Pennington relaxed in his seat again. A smug expression formed on his face.

"Yeah, that was a good one. With some interesting side benefits along the way," Pennington said with another grin, this one definitely heavy on the sleaze.

Side benefits? Was that how Pennington had viewed his relationship with Tami? Keaton forced himself not to make two fists and give the guy what he had coming to him.

"So, the side benefit. That would have been the woman you worked with?"

"Yeah. Nice enough, good body, but a bit too heavy on the good works and kindness for my liking. I prefer my women with a bit of mean in them."

"But mean is less malleable and a whole lot less trusting, right? You wouldn't have been able to fool a woman unless she trusted you."

"Sure, sure. Tami was a sweetheart. Enough to make your teeth rot, to be honest."

Again Keaton had to fight the urge to smash the guy into the next century. The way he spoke about Tami, the way he denigrated her. She deserved so much better than that.

"So she knew nothing about what you were doing?"

"Nah, of course not. If she'd had any idea she'd

have gone straight to the police. What's it to you, anyway? That doesn't have anything to do with us."

"True, I was just wondering if you'd had help pulling that off. If you had, I'd be withdrawing my offer. I don't want someone who needs someone else to make them successful. So tell me, with all you took from that charity you'd have been nicely set up in Nauru. What made my offer so attractive to you?"

Pennington shrugged. "Money is money, right? Can't ever have enough."

"And you have no scruples about how you get it?"

"None whatsoever."

The creep even looked proud of that fact.

"Sounds like you're just the kind of man I thought you were," Keaton said sardonically.

"I'm the man you want for the job, that's for sure. You give me those banking passwords and I can work wonders. Even split between the three of us, you said?"

Out of the corner of his eye, Keaton saw Hima and his partner rise from the table near them and walk over to Pennington. Hima put his hand firmly on Pennington's shoulder.

"Mark Pennington?"

"Hey, what's this?"

Pennington tried to rise from his seat but was firmly pushed back down by Hima, who was removing a set of cuffs from his belt.

"I'm arresting you in relation to the theft of two and a half millions dollars from the Our People, Our

Homes charity." He continued to read Pennington his rights then helped him from the chair.

Pennington turned to Keaton, his face feral. "You bastard! This was a setup?"

"It was," Keaton said with no small amount of satisfaction. "And your disgusting greed allowed you to fall for it hook, line and sinker."

Hima's partner began to escort Pennington to the front door, the other officers following in support. Hima stayed back a moment.

"Richmond, thanks for your help, and you, too, Jones." He shook both men's hands. "Let me get that gear off you and I'll be on my way."

Hima helped remove the wire from under Keaton's clothing.

"What's going to happen to him?" Keaton asked.

"He'll be charged and held pending a hearing. He's a flight risk so bail will be set high. A lot higher than what he'll have access to, anyway."

"And the money?"

"Steps are being taken to recover it as we speak. Eventually it'll be returned to the charity, but that'll take a while."

"Good, I'm glad to hear it," Keaton said.

After thanking Jones, he called a ride and traveled back to his apartment. By the time he arrived there, he was still pumped from the encounter. While not having actively enjoyed himself, there was an echoing sense of satisfaction in knowing he'd helped bring that thieving piece of work to justice. He hoped they threw the book at him. Stealing was bad enough, but stealing from a charity? That took a whole new level of low. And the way Pennington had unscrupulously used Tami was a burr under Keaton's skin. She deserved better than that. At least he'd helped clear her name with Our People, Our Homes.

That brought him to wondering how the charity would be able to continue to function without its operating capital until it was returned. He had no idea how long that would take. At least he knew that Tami would be cleared of any involvement. Pennington's words had fully exonerated her. And she'd know in due course. The police would be able to officially strike her from the investigation.

He wondered if that meant she'd stand a chance of getting a job back with them. Yes, she had breached their security process but it hadn't been a willful act and the funds would be returned, eventually. Maybe he could find out. Not that it was his business, but he wanted it to be. And he wanted to ensure that the charity didn't miss out, either. From his mother's work he knew how hard it was for these organizations to remain afloat unless they received grants. An idea began to percolate and he reached for his phone. It was time to pull out the big guns. His mom would know exactly what to do.

Tami set down the skein of lime-green yarn she'd offered to knit up for Keaton with a heart that felt as though it was made of lead. Try as she might, she couldn't bring herself to knit it up into a puppy jacket, despite that being her original intention. Keaton would have looked cute in one of her beanies, especially lime-green, she thought with a poignant smile.

Beside her, her mobile phone began to chirp. She recognized the number on the screen immediately. Our People, Our Homes. Who would be calling her from there, and why? She answered the call, surprised to hear the voice of the chairperson of the board on the other end.

"Tami, is that you?"

"Yes, Philippa. What can I do for you?"

"Well, actually this call is more about what we can do for you. First up, now that due processes have been followed with the investigation into yourself and Mark Pennington, we have reconsidered the termination of your employment."

"Reconsidered? We both know I was in breach of my employment and user agreements when I let Mark use my laptop."

The other woman made a shushing sound on the other end of the phone.

"That's true, your judgment regarding Mark Pennington was flawed, as was ours. However, we've received information from the police that clears you of any involvement in planning the theft of our operating funds."

"Seriously? That's fantastic!" Tami couldn't believe her ears. "How? What happened? Have you got the money back?"

Her questions tumbled one over the other and she heard Philippa laugh.

"I see you're still the same. It's good to know. We've missed you here. In answer to your questions, Mark was arrested three days ago and charged with theft. He's in custody. His statement to the police has cleared you from any wrongdoing."

"He came back? Why?"

"They didn't go into the exact details with me but they did say he was lured back in a sting operation. He had an ego, that man. He thought he could make it into the country and out again without the warrant for his arrest being activated."

"An offer?"

"Look, I don't know all the details, but suffice to say he's where he belongs, behind bars, and let's hope they keep him there for a very long time. Now, as to your last question, no, we don't have the money back, but we've been assured that after due process most of it will be returned to us. In the meantime, we've been granted a windfall from another source."

"How much of a windfall?"

"Five million dollars."

"Five—"

Tami's voice choked on the rest as emotion began to overwhelm her. She blinked back the tears that burned in her eyes. This was incredible. What they could do with this would make such a difference to so many people. But then she remembered, she was no longer a part of Our People, Our Homes. She would be forced to watch from the sidelines rather than be a true participant in the many great projects they could fund with this much money.

"It was totally unexpected," Philippa continued, "but there was one condition attached to it."

"A condition?"

"That you be reinstated to your previous position. Obviously that would be without the banking access you previously held, but your role would essentially still be the same."

Tami stiffened. Who would make such a stipulation, and why? Having been used not once but twice, recently, Tami was wary of the offer.

"Who made the donation?" she asked carefully.

"We don't know. It's been handled by a legal firm and the donor does not wish their name to be known. We're not about to look a gift horse in the mouth, however, so I would like to formally and officially invite you back, Tami."

Would they have invited her back if that condition hadn't been attached to the donation? she wondered. She'd accepted they had to fire her before, when she'd looked guilty, but this offer to return being tied to a large donation put her between a rock and a hard place. She didn't want to go back if it meant her earlier mistake would mean they'd constantly be monitoring her over her shoulder. Trust, once broken, was hard to win back, as she knew only too well.

And then there was her trust fund to consider. She'd been considering transferring it to Our People, Our Homes, anyway. She didn't need the money and she'd always wanted to do good with it rather than spend it on things that had no meaning to her. Just because she'd been exonerated from involvement with Mark's deception hadn't changed her desire to put that money to use where it would be most helpful.

"Tami?" Philippa prompted.

"I'd like to take a few days to think it over, if you don't mind."

"I understand," Philippa said. "Will you call me as soon as you've made your decision?"

"Of course."

Tami ended the call. She had a lot of thinking to do.

Thirteen

This was the kind of work that left her most fulfilled, Tami realized as she helped serve at the shelter she'd continued to volunteer at three nights a week. This was hands-on genuine support. All the administration she used to do had its purpose, but here she could really see and feel the difference she could make to someone else's life.

It was as different to her role at Richmond Developments as chalk was from cheese, and she didn't have to dress up in ridiculously expensive suits, either. Still, it had felt good, sometimes, to make that extra effort, especially when she'd seen a gleam of approval in Keaton's eyes. She clamped down on that thought as quickly as it hovered in the periphery of her mind. She couldn't allow herself to go down that road. She'd been doing so well in terms of getting on with her life. And, while she hadn't made her decision yet about whether or not to return to her role at Our People, Our Homes, she'd managed to keep busy with her volunteer work. By day she'd helped at the animal shelter, losing her heart to each and every abandoned dog or cat who'd been brought in. It was a no-kill shelter, but even so it was still, at times, heartbreaking work. And her evenings were either spent here or at home furiously working her needles and yarn into garments to donate.

But Tami knew all of this was merely a stopgap. She'd have to make a decision soon. She focused her attention back to passing out bread rolls to go with the stew that was on offer for dinner tonight. It was simple fare, but hearty. Tami smiled at the man in front of her. She only knew him as George, and knew he slept in doorways at night. Recently, he'd developed a hacking cough that worried her deeply. He'd refused medical help, but she was determined to try again to persuade him to attend a clinic. She was about to say something, but all of a sudden she felt a shift in the air. Several heads turned to the newcomer at the door.

All the hairs on the back of Tami's neck stood to attention and she slowly followed everyone's gaze. Keaton. She blinked, as if, after thinking about him and conjuring him out of thin air, she thought she could rid herself of his image on her retinas, but no, there he was and he was walking toward her.

"Expecting company?" George asked.

"No, I'm not."

"Looks like he's here to see you," the old man said with a raspy chuckle that set him off on another bout of coughing.

"George, you really need to let me take you to the clinic to get that cough seen to."

"Nah, I'll be fine."

He took his tray and turned away from her to join a group at one of the tables. Tami watched him as he settled down to eat. At least he still had an appetite, she observed. She turned back to the line of people waiting to be served and was shocked to see Keaton standing square in front of her.

"Why haven't you taken your old job back?" he demanded.

"What? No 'hello'? 'How are you, Tami?'" she responded and directed her attention to the young girl standing next to him and offered her a roll.

"Tami, please. Answer the question."

Slowly, it dawned on her that he must be behind the five million dollar donation. But why? A whole lot of questions burned on her tongue but she couldn't deal with this right now.

"I'm busy right now. If you want to talk to me, see if you can find yourself something to do and when my shift is ended, if you can wait that long, we'll talk."

"Fine," he answered in a clipped tone. "What can I do?"

Tami looked around, spying a small family who'd appeared with the newcomers this evening. They were seated against the wall, as if trying to be as inconspicuous as possible.

"Over there," she said, and nodded. "Jerome and his daughters need a hand. He can't feed both of them and himself at the same time. Go help him."

She was surprised when Keaton did just that.

"Miss, may I have a roll, please?"

An older lady, whose well-fitting fine woolen coat suggested she may have known better times, interrupted her and drew her attention back to her duty here. It grew busier from then on and it wasn't until the kitchen closed and she'd gone out back to help with the cleanup that she thought about Keaton again. When she came back into the main room, there he still was sitting by Jerome and with a sleeping one-year-old nestled in his arms. A group of men and women had gathered around them, all listening intently to whatever it was he was saying, but the instant he looked up and saw her standing in the kitchen doorway he said something to Jerome and handed off the baby back to her daddy.

Tami watched him as he walked toward her and she felt a frisson of awareness track down her spine. There was a lean, confident, animal grace to the way he moved and she wasn't the only one noticing it. There were appreciative glances from several of the people there.

"Are you free to talk now?" he asked.

"Thank you for staying with Jerome. It's his first night at the shelter. His wife died of influenza this winter and he lost his job because he had to stay home and care for the kids. And with the loss of his job they lost their accommodation, too. The baby, Lucy, has asthma and he's terrified she'll get sick."

"Do you know everything about all the people here?" he asked, cocking his head slightly.

"It's my business to know their business, Keaton. How can I best help them if I don't understand where they're coming from?"

"Good point. And, as to Jerome, I've offered him work on a small local restoration project that Logan's team is managing. Did you know he's a cabinetmaker by trade? He showed me photos of some of his work on his phone. We're always looking for craftsmen of his caliber. There's a reputable daycare facility nearby where he can leave the girls and I've offered him an advance on wages so he can secure accommodation for them all somewhere near to the project."

She was stunned. All that in one evening?

"Did he accept?"

"He did—he seemed excited about it. From what he's saying, it's the first time in a long time they've had something to look forward to." He looked back at Jerome, who was talking and smiling with the people around him. "I see what you mean about not just throwing money at a situation. You were right. People need the opportunity to take ownership of their lives."

"Not everyone wants assistance," Tami said softly, seeing the light of zeal in Keaton's eyes that was common in those new to volunteering. "But it's wonderful you could offer constructive help to someone who really needs it to get back on his feet."

"Which takes me back to my original question to you. Why haven't you taken your old job back?"

"That donation is from you?"

"Not me, personally, but our foundation, yes."

"Why put strings on it? If you were so moved as to make such a huge contribution to Our People, Our Homes, why put all the responsibility of whether they receive the money, or not, back on to my shoulders. To be honest, a donation with a condition is not a donation at all, is it? It's a manipulation and I won't be manipulated. I've been there, I've jumped through other people's hoops and I don't like it. I'm my own person. I make my own decisions. I will not be coerced."

She realized the shelter had grown silent as her voice had grown louder and everyone around them was staring. It didn't matter, she thought, as her cheeks flamed. The words needed to be said. A slow clap started at the back of the room, soon joined by more and more people applauding. The tips of Keaton's ears turned red and he turned to raise one hand in acknowledgement and silent apology for what they'd overheard.

"Look, can we talk somewhere that's a little more private? You've misinterpreted my intentions."

"Really? And tell me, what were your intentions?"

"Please, Tami. Somewhere private?"

"Go on, Tami, give the guy a break. He looks

pretty and he smells nice," one of the older female regulars said from behind Keaton.

"You think so?" Tami answered with a wry grin. "You can have him if you want him, Sally. He's single."

The woman cackled in response. "Hell, no. Too high-maintenance for me!"

Tami saw Keaton's shoulder sag in relief and she couldn't help but grin. To give him credit, at least he hadn't run for the door, yet.

"Okay," she relented. "There's a coffee shop around the corner. Would that do?"

Keaton looked at her. "Are you all finished up here?"

"Yes, why?"

"How were you planning to get home?"

"Parking here is difficult so I took a bus. I was going to call a ride to get home."

"Why don't I see you home? We can talk there."

Tami mulled over his suggestion. What difference did it make, in the long run? She'd say what she had to say, and he'd hopefully listen. Then he'd go away again. She wondered how many more times her heart would have to be torn apart by this man, by either leaving him or watching him leave her.

"Fine. Let's go then."

She grabbed her coat and followed him out the door after bidding everyone good-night. They walked a short distance in the dark, wet streets to where he'd parked his car under a streetlight.

"You were lucky to get a spot here," she commented as he held the door open for her.

"I had to drive around the block a few times, but I was prepared to wait. I needed to see you."

Tami merely grunted a noncommittal response and busied herself putting on her seat belt as Keaton closed her door and got in on the other side. They didn't speak as they drove out to her home on the outskirts of town, and after they alighted from the car Keaton followed her down the path to her front door. Once they were inside she led him to her small sitting room and gestured for him to take a seat.

"Can I offer you anything? Tea? Coffee?"

"No, thank you, please just sit with me." When she'd settled on an easy chair he continued. "Look, you got me all wrong on the donation. I know you lost your position at Our People, Our Homes because of Pennington and your involvement with him. I just wanted to ensure that they made your job available to you again now that your name is cleared."

"How did you know that my name is cleared?" she asked.

He firmed his lips a moment before speaking again. "I was involved in the sting that brought Pennington back to the States. A man like that is motivated by money, lots of money, so with the help of the police, I dangled an obscene sum in front of him as bait and he fell for it."

"But why would you do that? You had nothing to do with him, or the charity. What did you stand to gain?"

"Nothing, personally. But you stood to gain your

reputation back. You deserved to have your name cleared of all and any guilt or suspicion."

She looked at him in surprise and shook her head slowly. "That's not what you thought a short while back. May I remind you of the damages claim your company has against me?"

"Our lawyers have been instructed to drop it. You should get confirmation on that from your lawyer tomorrow. I was so angry with you for what you'd done to us at Richmond Developments I was determined to make you pay. That said, it was unfair of me to treat you the way I did and not to listen or try to understand why you were forced to do what you did. I understand that now and I plan to try harder to listen first before jumping to conclusions. I hope you can help me with that and that you'll find it in your very warm and generous heart to forgive me for my behavior."

"Warm and generous?"

"I've watched you, Tami. I know that at your core you are the most incredible, beautiful, loving woman I think I've ever known. And you're like that with everyone you meet. Whether it's the people at the shelter, or your work colleagues, or even a total stranger in the street. You exude warmth and caring. You deserve far better than the way Mark Pennington treated you, or the way I treated you. That's why I wanted you to get your old job back and I wanted them to have sufficient motivation to ensure they took you back. I understand how shaky things were there financially after the money was stolen and while most of what Pennington stole will be returned to them, it's going to take time. Time they probably did not have. So the Richmond Foundation took up the slack. That's all. Putting a proviso on the donation was for your sake, not to manipulate you, but to give you back what was taken from you."

"Five million dollars is a lot of slack, Keaton."

"We looked further into the charity. It does really good things, but like all charities they're hamstrung by financial constraints. We think we've found a way forward where we can possibly use some of our construction as a method of providing the low-cost, low-interest housing you discussed with me in Sedona, and provide jobs for skilled workers on hard times. Working with Our People, Our Homes is a viable way for us to do this."

"That's really great news, and I'll give serious consideration to resuming my old role. I miss it. But I'm not sure it's the right thing to do."

"Well, you could always come back and work with me," he said with a smile.

"No, I couldn't. I don't want to go anywhere where people will always be second-guessing my integrity."

Keaton looked at her as comprehension dawned. For the first time he really understood the toll this entire chain of events, started by that lowlife Pennington, had taken on her. She was right. Because of Pennington, her integrity had been grossly undermined, and he'd added to that.

"Tami, I'm so sorry."

"Don't you see, Keaton. In forcing Our People, Our Homes to take me back, I'll never know whether I'm there because I'm worth it, or because you made them do it. I know you think you were trying to help, but you've only made it worse for me."

"I was trying to help," he insisted. "And we can certainly make the donation unconditional."

But he knew it was too late. The damage was done. And, considering the way Pennington and her father and who knew who else had treated her, he knew why it was so important to Tami to feel valued. Another idea took shape in his mind.

"I have a suggestion and I want you to consider it carefully before giving me an answer."

"More manipulation, Keaton?" she asked wearily.

"No, an opportunity for something new. The Richmond Foundation, Our People, Our Homes and Richmond Developments will need someone to act as the coordinator for the new affordable-homes initiative. I don't see why that shouldn't be you, if you wanted the role. It would give you the opportunity to expand on the organizational skills you've already proven you excel at, while allowing you the hands-on involvement with the people you're so passionate about caring for. You're far better-suited to that position than anyone we could appoint internally from Richmond."

Her expression changed and he saw a glow of hope light up in those beautiful hazel eyes of hers.

"You'd offer that to me?" she asked, still sounding unsure. "But you have no reason to trust me. We both know that."

Keaton sat forward in his chair and reached for her hands, holding them both in his, then stared directly into her eyes.

"I understand why you did what you did, Tami. And I forgive you, totally and absolutely. I'll admit, it took me a while—too long a while, to be honest— but I know now it was your compassionate heart that led you to take the steps you did. I'm sorry you were forced to do that. I'm sorry your father used you that way and I'm sorry that a man like Pennington put you in a position where you felt you had to turn to your father for help."

"None of that was your fault," she said, pulling back.

He felt the loss of her touch as if she'd slammed a door in his face, but he wasn't going to give up. Not yet, maybe not ever.

"No, but my reaction to the situation could definitely have been better. I did what I could to bring Pennington to justice, for you, Tami."

"But, why?"

"Because…" Keaton took her hands again. "I would have done the same thing for any person that I loved. I had to bring Pennington back to the US no matter the cost because of what he'd done to you and to Our People, Our Homes. He had to pay for what he's done and he will pay, dearly. You weren't his first mark, Tami, and you wouldn't have been his last. He had to be stopped. Anyway, that's what

I needed to say. I'll go now. But, please, think about my offer, okay?"

He got up and began to walk toward the front door, but stopped when he felt Tami's hand on his shoulder. He turned around. There was an incredulous expression on her face.

"Did you just say you love me?"

He smiled. "Well, yeah. I love you, Tami Wilson. More than I'll ever be able to express in words, so I had to do it with actions. Will you forgive me for being so arrogant about everything? For not listening? For not trusting what my own eyes had told me about you? For not trying to understand you better?"

"Of course, I forgive you, Keaton, not that I believe I have anything to forgive you for—you are exactly who you are and I love you for all of it. I think I've loved you since you were so patient with me on the tandem zip line and taught me then to trust you. Knowing what my father wanted me to do to Richmond Developments tore me up inside, all the more so because I continued to learn about what an incredible man you are. Intelligent, mostly patient, strong and kind. And, I have it on good authority that you smell good, too," she said with a chuckle.

"Mostly patient?" he asked with a crooked smile.

"You know what I mean," she said.

Tami slipped her arms around his waist and cuddled in close for a moment before stepping back and taking his face in her hands and gently pulling him down toward her. He needed no encouragement. He'd been craving her taste, her touch, from the second he'd woken on the morning after they'd first made love. The morning he'd sent her out of his life. Their lips met, sealed and ignited a conflagration of need inside him. Her also, judging by the enthusiasm with which she returned the embrace.

He pressed her up against a closed door and lifted her hands above her head, stepping in so close to her that his hips met with hers. He pressed against her and felt her groan into his mouth. He dragged his lips from hers and burned a trail of kisses from her mouth to her jaw, then down her neck.

"Bedroom," she growled in a hoarse voice. "Behind me, the door, open it."

He didn't need to be told twice. Keaton twisted the doorknob and pushed open the door to the darkened room, then turned around so she could walk him backward toward the bed. As he did so, she began to reach for the buttons on his shirt, the buckle of his belt, his zipper. By the time they reached her bed, he was more than half-naked and he kicked off his shoes and shucked off the last of his clothing before helping her off with her jeans and the soft sweater she wore.

There were no niceties about their urgency. Only need, demand, give-and-take. She pushed him back onto the bed and straddled him. He reached for her breasts, cupping them in his hands and squeezing gently. Her thighs tightened around his and he felt the wet heat of her body against his skin. He squeezed her breasts again, this time pulling gently at her nipples with his thumbs and forefingers, and was rewarded with a moan that seemed to come from deep inside her.

Tami bent down then, and began a thorough exploration of his body. Taking her time to nuzzle and lick and kiss and, yes, bite her way from his neck to his abdomen. When she got to his belly button, she looked up at him with a wicked grin.

"Sally's right. You do smell good. *All* of you smells good."

He laughed but it was a strangled sound. "Can we please leave Sally out of the bedroom?"

She chuckled again and Keaton decided he could very well get drunk on the sound. "I will if you will."

She bent her head again and took his erection into her mouth. His entire body started in reflex to the warm, wet shock of her possession of him. He forced himself to relax, to enjoy, to give in to the sensations she wrought from him, and when he climaxed, she took that from him, too. Taking her time to give him the deepest of pleasures while he ached to give her her own.

She shifted again so her body was over his and he wrapped his arms around her tight. Right now, he never wanted to let her go, ever again. He knew that this was more than a fleeting kind of love. This was something he wanted, with her, forever. They stayed together like that until he felt his heart rate return to normal, until he felt his body stir to life again. He rolled her over and hovered over her, returning the pleasure she'd given him, taking his time to savor the very special taste of her skin, the heat of her body, the texture of every inch of her.

Tami was squirming beneath him when he felt her reach for the top drawer on her bedside cabinet. She dragged it open and grabbed a foil packet from inside.

"Now, Keaton. Please. No more playing around. I want you, inside me. Filling me. Loving me."

"Of course. Whatever you want. Always."

He sheathed himself and positioned himself at her entrance, then forced himself to take it slowly, entering her body and feeling her welcome him, inch by slow inch. When he was buried to the hilt he stopped, allowed them both to relish the depth of their connection. Her arms were up, her hands beside her head, and he laced his fingers with hers and bent down to kiss her. A long, wet, thorough kiss that left them both breathless.

"I love you, Tami Wilson. I'm going to love you for the rest of my life," he promised solemnly.

And then he began to move. At first slowly and then, as his movements stoked the flames of their desire, faster and faster until, in a swoop of pleasure, they reached their peak together. Exhilaration flooded him and he felt her body's reaction to the joy they'd just given one another. Felt the pulse that beat through her, felt her shake and buck gently beneath him until her body suddenly relaxed and he allowed himself to settle into her before gently rolling them both onto their sides.

He looked at her in the semidark. The room lit

only by the light from the hallway. Both of them panting. He could feel the light sheen of perspiration on her body and tracked the shape of her face with one hand.

"I mean it, Tami. I love you more than I ever knew was possible. Will you help me to grow our relationship into something that will last both our lifetimes?"

She reached a shaking hand to cup his face and closed the small distance between them to kiss him.

"Keaton Richmond, I'd be honored to do that with you. Yes, my answer is, yes. To everything. To spending the rest of my life with you, to loving you forever. To being the example to our children that they will deserve."

"Our kids, I like the sound of that." He kissed her back. "The day I saw you in the office for the first time, I wondered what the hell I was letting myself in for. Now I know. Thank you for remaining true to who you are and I promise I will remain true to you every day I draw breath."

"Oh, Keaton, thank you. I will treasure your words, and you, for the rest of my days."

"I never realized it until you came into my life, that you're all I ever wanted," he said solemnly. "I guess I should thank your father for that."

She laughed and he felt her whole body shake.

"Yeah, I don't think so. I'd like to imagine we'd have come to each other eventually."

"Yeah," he agreed and tightened his arms around her some more. "I can't wait to see what our future brings."

"It's going to be like our zip line ride," she murmured, snuggling into his chest and inhaling deeply. "Challenging, a little bit terrifying, but overall it's going to be absolutely amazing."

And it was.

* * * * *

*Don't miss
the next story in
Yvonne Lindsay's
Clashing Birthrights series,
available June 2021
from Harlequin Desire.*

COMING NEXT MONTH FROM

⒣HARLEQUIN

DESIRE

Available March 9, 2021

#2791 AT THE RANCHER'S PLEASURE
Texas Cattleman's Club: Heir Apparent • by Joss Wood
Runaway groom Brett Harston was Royal's favorite topic until Sarabeth Edmonds returned. Banished years before by her ex-husband, she's determined to reclaim her life and reputation. But a spontaneous kiss meant to rile up town gossips unleashes a passionate romance neither can ignore...

#2792 CRAVING A REAL TEXAN
The Texas Tremaines • by Charlene Sands
Grieving CEO Cade Tremaine retreats to his family's cabin and finds gorgeous chef Harper Dawn. She's wary and hiding her identity after rejecting a televised proposal, but their spark is immediate. Will the Texan find a second chance at love, or will Harper's secret drive him away?

#2793 WAKING UP MARRIED
The Bourbon Brothers • by Reese Ryan
One passionate Vegas night finds bourbon executive Zora Abbott married to her friend Dallas Hamilton. To protect their reputations after their tipsy vows go viral, they agree to stay married for one year. But their fake marriage is realer and hotter than they could've imagined!

#2794 HOW TO LIVE WITH TEMPTATION
by Fiona Brand
Billionaire Tobias Hunt has always believed the beautiful Allegra Mallory was only after his money. Now, forced to live and work together, she claims a fake fiancé to prove she isn't interested. But with sparks flying, Tobias wants what he can no longer have...

#2795 AFTER HOURS ATTRACTION
404 Sound • by Kianna Alexander
After finding out his ex embezzled funds, recording COO Gage Woodson has sworn off workplace romance. But when he's stranded with his assistant, Ainsley Voss, on a business trip, their chemistry is too hot to ignore. Will they risk their working relationship for something more?

#2796 HIS PERFECT FAKE ENGAGEMENT
Men of Maddox Hill • by Shannon McKenna
When a scandal jeopardizes playboy CEO Drew Maddox's career, he proposes a fake engagement to his brilliant and philanthropic friend Jenna Sommers to revitalize his reputation and fund her efforts. But as passion takes over, can this bad boy reform his ways for her?

SPECIAL EXCERPT FROM

(H) HARLEQUIN
DESIRE

When a scandal jeopardizes playboy CEO Drew Maddox's career, he proposes a fake engagement to his brilliant and philanthropic friend Jenna Sommers to revitalize his reputation and fund her efforts. But as passion takes over, can this bad boy reform his ways for her?

Read on for a sneak peek at
His Perfect Fake Engagement
by New York Times *bestselling author Shannon McKenna!*

Drew pulled her toward the big Mercedes SUV idling at the curb. "Here's your ride," he said. "We still on for tonight? I wouldn't blame you if you changed your mind. The paparazzi are a huge pain in the ass. Like a weather condition. Or a zombie horde."

"I'm still game," she said. "Let `em do their worst."

That got her a smile that touched off fireworks at every level of her consciousness.

For God's sake. Get a grip, girl.

"I'll pick you up for dinner at eight fifteen," he said. "Our reservation at Peccati di Gola is at eight forty-five."

"I'll be ready," she promised.

"Can I put my number into your phone, so you can text me your address?"

"Of course." She handed him her phone and waited as he tapped the number into it. He hit Call and waited for the ring.

"There," she said, taking her phone back. "You've got me now."

"Lucky me," he murmured. He glanced back at the photographers, still blocked by three security men at the door, still snapping photos. "You're no delicate flower, are you?"

"By no means," she assured him.

"I like that," he said. He'd already opened the car door for her, but as she was about to get inside, he pulled her swiftly back up again and covered her mouth with his.

His kiss was hotter than the last one. Deliberate, demanding. He pressed her closer, tasting her lips.

Oh. Wow. He tasted amazing. Like fire, like wind. Like sunlight on the ocean. She dug her fingers into the massive bulk of his shoulders, or tried to. He was so thick and solid. Her fingers slid helplessly over the fabric of his jacket. They could get no grip.

His lips parted hers. The tip of his tongue flicked against hers, coaxed her to open, to give herself up. To yield to him. His kiss promised infinite pleasure in return. It demanded surrender on a level so deep and primal, she responded instinctively.

She melted against him with a shudder of emotion that was absolutely unfaked.

Holy crap. Panic pierced her as she realized what was happening. He'd kissed her like he meant it, and she'd responded in the same way. As naturally as breathing.

She was so screwed.

Jenna pulled away, shaking. She felt like a mask had been pulled off. That he could see straight into the depths of her most private self.

And Drew helped her into the car and gave her a reassuring smile and a friendly wave as the car pulled away, like it was no big deal. As if he hadn't just tongue-kissed her passionately in front of a crowd of photographers and caused an inner earthquake.

Her lips were still glowing. They tingled from the contact.

She couldn't let her mind stray down this path. She was a means to an end.

It was Drew Maddox's nature to be seductive. He was probably that way with every woman he talked to. He probably couldn't help himself. Not even if he tried.

She had to keep that fact firmly in mind.

All. The. Time.

Don't miss what happens next in…
His Perfect Fake Engagement
by New York Times *bestselling author Shannon McKenna!*

Available March 2021 wherever
Harlequin Desire books and ebooks are sold.

Harlequin.com

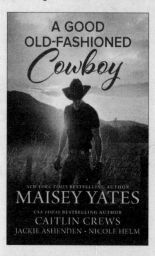